"Stealing Jenny is a gripping novel *filled with engaging characters, a* compelling mystery and a message which underscores the precious dignity of life. I literally couldn't put it down and give Stealing Jenny my highest recommendation."
Lisa M. Hendey, Founder of CatholicMom.com and author of "A Book of Saints for Catholic Moms"

"Stealing Jenny will keep you on the edge of your seat and probably destroy your sleep pattern as you stay up to find out what happens. But beyond being a great suspense, it's also an excellent example of morals in action and family life redeemed. As a fan of Ellen Gable's work already, I'm now officially getting a t-shirt!"
Sarah Reinhard, author, "Welcome Baby Jesus: Advent and Christmas Reflections for Families"

"Ellen Gable is a masterful storyteller. Stealing Jenny is a smoothly written, chilling tale of gripping suspense. There are terrifying moments and heart-wrenching moments. Catholic faith and hope are tested. Above all, the sacredness and privilege of precious new life is made indisputably evident. I never wanted it to end!"
Therese Heckenkamp, Traditional Catholic Novels.com

"Stealing Jenny is my favorite kind of fiction: a thought-provoking psychological suspense novel in its own right, with a life-affirming message that adds even more to its depth. Another finely-plotted story and a cast of very real and well-drawn characters which highlight Ellen Gable's ability to write beautiful Catholic fiction in any genre."
Krisi Keley, author, "On the Soul of a Vampire," and "Pro Luce Habere"

"I could not put it down! Stealing Jenny, the latest novel from Ellen Gable (Emily's Hope, In Name Only), is the gripping fictional story of a desperate woman who plots to kidnap pregnant Jenny Callahan in order to steal her unborn baby. I highly recommend this book."
Donna Piscitelli, award-winning author

"Stealing Jenny is a real page turner of a novel that will keep you on the edge of your seat till the end. I was especially inspired by the characters' perseverance and faith, which helps them navigate the nightmare their family must confront and overcome. Highly recommended reading."
Christopher Blunt, author, "Passport"

Stealing Jenny

A Novel

Ellen Gable

Nick,
Enjoy!
God bless,
Ellie

Ellen Gable Hrkach

Full Quiver Publishing, Pakenham, Ontario

STEALING JENNY
copyright by Full Quiver Publishing
PO Box 244
Pakenham, Ontario
K0A 2X0

ISBN Number: 978-0-9736736-2-3
Printed and bound in USA

Cover design by
James and Ellen Hrkach

NATIONAL LIBRARY OF CANADA CATALOGUING IN
PUBLICATION

Gable, Ellen 1959 -
In Name Only/ Ellen Gable

Stealing Jenny has been awarded the
Catholic Writers' Guild Seal of Approval 2011

Books by Ellen Gable:

Emily's Hope: Honorable Mention, Independent
Publisher Book Awards (IPPY) Religious Fiction 2006
Catholic Writers' Guild Seal of Approval 2009
www.emilyshope.com

In Name Only: Gold Medal Winner, Independent Publisher Book
Awards (IPPY) Religious Fiction 2010
Catholic Writers' Guild Seal of Approval 2009
Amazon Kindle Bestseller Top 100 (Religious Fiction)
www.innameonly.ca

Edited by Ellen Gable:
Come My Beloved: **Inspiring Stories of Catholic Courtship**
(with Kathy Cassanto)
Catholic Writers' Guild Seal of Approval 2011
Amazon Kindle Bestseller (Inspirational Books)
www.comemybeloved.com

For my sister, Laurie
Sister Elizabeth Grace

"In God I trust; I will not be afraid.
What can man do to me?"
Psalm 56:11

August 4th

One more baby to hold in her arms. That's all Jenny Callahan wanted. After three heartbreaking miscarriages, every twinge and cramp at the beginning of this pregnancy had caused her to fear for her unborn child's life. But now, with less than six weeks until her due date, she felt like she was "home free."

Jenny didn't initially notice the swirling dark red fluid on the shower floor under her large pregnant stomach. When she finally did see the bright explosion of crimson in the water, she stifled a scream and started to shake uncontrollably. The only person home was three-year-old Caleb, who was sitting in front of the television watching a Barney DVD. Jenny's husband, Tom, and their four daughters were an hour away at the movie theater in Ottawa. She quickly turned off the shower, stuffed a towel between her legs and pulled on her robe. She began to hyperventilate and had to will herself to calm down. *I must call Mom.* Her mother arrived within minutes and whisked her and Caleb off to the hospital. During the entire five-minute journey, she begged God to allow Little Buddy to be born safely. Her baby was in real jeopardy, considering the blood which had already soaked through the towel and was now seeping onto the seat. The mineral scent was sickening. *Please, God, I'll do anything you ask of me, just let Little Buddy be okay.* Her mother kept saying "It'll be fine," but that's what mothers are supposed to say. Moments later, Jenny breathed a sigh of relief when the ultrasound revealed the baby's obvious heartbeat and movement. However, the doctor cautioned, she would have to remain on bed rest in the hospital for a day or so until they could stop the bleeding.

One

September 8th
One month later

Jenny knelt in front of the toilet, her protruding stomach pressed against the porcelain bowl. Her toddler stared quizzically at her.

"Momma 'kay?" Caleb asked.

"Uh-huh. I'm just. . ." She emptied the contents of her stomach, straightened, then exhaled.

"Yuck." Caleb leaned in, but kept a safe distance away.

She didn't particularly like the nausea, but welcomed it because her doctor said that it meant that Little Buddy was still safe within her womb.

Motherhood and pregnancy already had their usual challenges, especially with five small children. But when she first held her daughter, Christine, in her arms, she realized that this was her purpose in life: to be a mom.

The forced bed rest for most of the past month had been difficult, to say the least. Thankfully, a week ago, the doctor gave her permission to do simple housework and pick up the kids from the bus stop, but advised her to remain off her feet most of the time.

She reached for the hand towel on the counter and wiped her mouth.

"Don't like that." Caleb's small hand patted her head. "Kay, Mom?"

"Yes, I'm okay." She pushed herself up and stared at her reflection in the bathroom mirror. Some pregnant women glowed, but pregnancy usually brought out the worst in her, from the oily hair to the slight acne to the constant green tinge. At least her maternity shirt was bright and pretty with blue and white flowers.

"Come on, Caleb." She took hold of her son's hand and

led him into the kitchen for a snack, then noticed that he hadn't finished his grilled cheese sandwich. Now that her stomach was empty, the half-eaten lunch looked appetizing. She ate a couple bites, felt queasy again, then decided against finishing it.

She got a box of crackers from the cupboard and gave a handful to Caleb, who shoved them in his mouth.

Dirty dishes were stacked on the counter. She knew that she ought to wash them, but at this time of the day, her body cried out for rest more than anything else. Besides, the doctor advised her to stay off her feet as much as possible.

Leaning against the sliding doors, Jenny stared at the spacious back yard. It was a beautiful, summer-like day and she breathed in the fresh air. One of the neat things about pregnancy was the heightened sense of smell, although that could also be a disadvantage, depending on the scent.

Behind her, Bootsie barked to go outside. Jenny slid open the patio door and the beagle scampered away.

She took her son's hand, sat him in front of the television and turned on a Blues Clues DVD.

Jenny lowered herself onto the sofa, her heavy pregnant body sinking into the cushions. Immediately, the dog began to whine and scratch at the back door. She sighed, pushed herself up and trudged across the living room and kitchen to open the sliding glass doors. The dog ran inside.

The clock on the wall chimed that it was quarter to three. In half an hour, the girls would be arriving at the bus stop. The new school year had been in session for the past week. Jenny had been hoping that this year she could persuade Chris to walk her sisters home the one and a half blocks. Unfortunately, Chris had a fear of walking alone since she heard her classmates talking about a girl who was abducted in Toronto. She tried to reassure her daughter that that sort of thing didn't happen in their small community, but Christine wouldn't hear any of it.

Jenny made her way to the sofa once more, dropped onto the soft cushions and laid her head back.

Closing her eyes, she began to drift off. As if on cue, her unborn baby stretched and kicked her in the ribs. "Little Buddy, cut it out!" 'Little Buddy' was what Tom had called all their babies while they were in the womb. It was, of course, the nickname Skipper had called Gilligan on the old 60's sitcom Gilligan's Island.

During her last ultrasound, the baby wasn't in a position to see its gender. Tom was certain that it was another boy, although Jenny didn't have an inclination either way.

As she suspected, when her husband had informed his mother, Doris, about this latest pregnancy eight months ago, the woman had harsh words for them. Jenny stood silent beside Tom, listening to the entire exchange, while her mother-in-law spoke as if Jenny wasn't there.

"You're asking for trouble."

"Trouble?"

"Jenny's already had three miscarriages in a row."

"Call us stubborn, Mom. We both want another child."

"Can't you just be grateful for the five you have?"

"We are grateful, Mom."

"Well, it's irresponsible."

"We want a large family and we can afford them. You and dad had the four of us, didn't you?"

"Nobody can afford that many kids these days," Doris had said. "And I didn't have the problems your wife has."

Jenny and Tom had remained silent while Doris continued. "Besides, your house is too small."

Later, when they told his dad, he had simply been quiet, but he shook his head the entire time with the odd "tsk" coming out of his mouth. Tom looked a lot like his dad, the older man's thinning red hair fading to gray and his fair skin wrinkled. Despite the similarity, his father rarely smiled.

At work, Tom had become a laughingstock, enduring such barbs as "Don't you know what causes that?" and "Can't you control yourself?" Tom confided that he had acted as if he was going along with their jokes, while suffering inwardly. Jenny had wanted to march right down there and tell his co-workers that Tom had more self-control in his little finger than they had in their entire bodies.

Jenny stole a glance at the clock as she rested on the couch. Five minutes to three. Just enough time for a ten-minute nap before she had to leave to pick up the girls at the bus stop.

Two

In her living room, Denise Kramer peered out the window at the bus stop across the street. She took the last drag of her cigarette, then crushed it in the ashtray while slowly exhaling. Jenny Callahan would soon be traipsing up the street to pick up her daughters at the bus stop.

She first noticed Jenny four months ago at the veterinary clinic where Denise worked as a vet tech. Denise couldn't stand the way Jenny paraded her big stomach in front of her, lording it over her that she was pregnant and Denise was not. Later that week, Denise was alone for a few hours working at the office doing treatments for the post-op animals. She took out Bootsie Callahan's file and discovered that Jenny lived only two blocks away. Better yet, Jenny's kids caught the school bus right across the street from her.

During the ensuing weeks, Denise occasionally parked across the street and watched them through the front bay window in their living room which was rarely curtained off. She couldn't stand their quaint happy family with their quaint little house and their quaint laughing children. No family could possibly be *that* happy.

Over the past four months, she spent time searching online to find out more about the Callahans. The more she studied them, the more she hated them: the kind of couple who just looked at each other and became pregnant.

Denise, on the other hand, had tried for years to get pregnant with her husband, Lou. Fertility drugs, three failed in vitro attempts and still no baby. The last straw was when the adoption agency turned them down, saying that Denise's smoking, and her 'questionable' psychological assessment precluded them from placing any babies in their care. Lou finally left, telling her that she was "obsessed" with having a baby.

Denise soon began to share the "news" with her co-workers, neighbors and cousin that she was pregnant. When asked, she told them that she had decided to attempt in vitro again without Lou and this time, it worked.   Many celebrities and Octomom had proven that women can have babies without a significant other.   Who needed fathers anyway?

Except she wouldn't be trying in-vitro again; she had a better plan.

At work, she darted off to the bathroom several times a day and pretended that she was sick, even making gagging sounds to complete the illusion. Although she was already somewhat round in the middle, she ordered a rubber pregnant belly (with inserts for making it bigger) from a theater costume place online and finally began to wear maternity clothes.

She slipped her hand inside her shirt and scratched her stomach under the rubber belly as she kept watch in front her window. It was an annoyance to wear, but Denise relished the extra attention from co-workers, her neighbor and even perfect strangers who smiled at her.

Last week, she explained to her boss that she was going to take maternity leave early because she was having problems with the pregnancy.

Dr. Eastman, the veterinarian who had just returned to work after having given birth to her baby boy a few months previous, seemed uncharacteristically sympathetic.

Denise planned to spend most of her time watching the Callahans. As well, she needed this time to finish planning.

Operation Baby Plan A was to wait until Jenny was within a week or two of giving birth and kidnap her from the bus stop. She overheard Jenny tell the receptionist at the vet's office that her due date was September 20th, meaning Denise would have to act within the next few days.

What made this location so ideal was that a huge field ran parallel to Denise's house and was the only house with a clear view. This was also one of the quietest neighborhoods in Sutherland, with many of the mothers, including Loretta, her landlord from next door, working during the day.

After the baby was born, Denise planned to dye her hair, probably blonde, and assume another alias. She had already purchased the fake I.D.s including an Ontario health card using her middle name and maiden name, Joanne Cox, as well as fake Ontario license plates. She also ordered a fake birth certificate for the baby. She decided to get it with one of those either/or first names, Taylor. Those fake I.D's and the car license plates cost her a huge sum but would be essential to have when she put her plan into action. Nowadays, anything could be purchased online for a price.

If, by some chance, Jenny gave birth before Denise could kidnap her, Operation Baby Plan B would be put into place.

She lit up another cigarette and kept vigil at the window.

With a whoosh and the smell of engine exhaust, the school bus pulled up and the Callahan girls got out. Where was Jenny? The oldest girl looked bewildered and even glanced across the street at Denise standing at the window. Denise moved behind the curtain and out of sight, but peeked out to watch them. The girl leaned down and whispered to her younger sisters, then straightened and took hold of each of their hands. As they walked away, Denise clenched her fists. *What if Jenny has already gone into labor?*

Don't panic, she calmed herself. *I must find out what's happened to Jenny.*

Denise came out of her house and followed the girls home, staying far behind and on the opposite side of the street. Once, the oldest girl looked back and Denise looked away, trying to appear nonchalant, then ducked behind a car until they were nearly home.

When the four little girls reached their house, Denise moved forward. Once the girls were inside, she stood up and watched the scene through the large bay window in front.

Jenny was on the couch, the little boy watching television. Denise relaxed against the telephone pole, relieved. Tomorrow she would set her plan in motion.

* * *

"Mom, we're home!" Christine's voice woke Jenny. She opened her eyes and sat upright as all four girls came into the living room. "How come you didn't meet us at the bus stop? I was scared when I didn't see you. I saw a lady looking strangely at us from the house across the street from the bus stop. She really creeped me out. I think I saw her following us home too." Chris was scowling and leaning over her. Her oldest daughter was the only Callahan child who hadn't inherited some form of Tom's red hair. With her long brown hair, she reminded Jenny of herself at that age.

"Honey, I'm sorry. I fell asleep. Thanks for walking the girls home. A lady looking strangely at you?"

Her daughter nodded.

Jenny took a deep breath, then exhaled. Chris was a worrier and a little on the paranoid side.

"You know, people are allowed to look out their windows and walk on the street."

"Yeah, well, she looked kinda familiar."

"Familiar?"

"Yeah, but I can't remember where I've seen her before."

"Well, if she lives near the bus stop, you may have seen her in the neighborhood."

"I don't think so." Chris pulled a paper out of her backpack. "Hey, I got 100 on my spelling test." She held it in front of Jenny's face.

"That's fantastic, Chris."

"Hi Mommy," said Callie and Cassie, in unison.

"Hi, girls."

"Mom, look at my drawing," Chloe, her six year old, said, as she placed it on Jenny's lap.

"That's beautiful, honey."

* * *

"Jen, sit down. I'll wash the dishes tonight. You're supposed to be off your feet." Jenny's husband, Tom, was already piling dishes into the dishwasher.

"I know, but you cooked supper too. And the doctor said I could do simple tasks like the dishes and walking the girls to the bus stop."

"You should be taking it easy. Sit down and talk to me while I do the dishes." He was gently lowering her to the chair. He flipped the dish towel over his shoulder and washed a pot while whistling the tune from Gilligan's Island. He wore her apron with the fading letters of "Mom's Apron: Please Wipe Nose Below Line" with a red line low on the garment. A small darkish stain had taken up residence below the line last summer when she had made blackberry jam. Jenny cringed when she recalled the last time her mother-in-law came for dinner. Doris kept staring at the line and the stain, wondering if Jenny really allowed her kids to wipe their noses on her apron.

Tom glanced at her and winked.

"You look adorable in that apron," Jenny teased.

"Don't I know it."

These were the times that she wanted to drag him upstairs to the bed and make mad passionate love to him. She looked down at her large stomach and sighed.

"I should at least dry the dishes." She stood up.

"Uh-uh. No drying, no nothing. You need to rest. You've got two birthdays to prepare for."

"Two?"

Tom was smiling at her with raised eyebrows.

"Oh, right, my birthday." Jenny hugged her husband from behind and kissed his back.

"I wish you were feeling better."

"How did you know I wasn't feeling well?"

He turned and held her at arm's length. "It could be the green tinge emanating from your body. . .or perhaps it's the dark circles under your eyes. Seriously, Hon, you look exhausted."

"I wish we could. . .you know," she whispered.

He pulled her to an embrace. "Me too, but you know what the doctor said: none of that until after the birth."

Three

September 9th

The first noise Jenny heard the next morning was a bird chirping outside the bedroom window. It was a beautiful, warm day. Thankful that she had woken before the alarm, Jenny felt more energy than she'd had in weeks and quickly dressed in a navy blue and white maternity top and stretch jeans. Perhaps she was experiencing the "nesting instinct." With only six days before her scheduled C-section next week, she still had much to accomplish. It didn't help that her aunt had suffered a stroke and her mother had to fly out to Saskatchewan to be with her. After enduring the heartache of losing three babies through miscarriage, Little Buddy would be in her arms in less than a week.

Downstairs in the kitchen, she mixed together a batch of cranberry muffins and placed them in the oven. The benefit of living in a smaller home was that you could hear what was going on in any part of the house. She heard Tom's alarm, then waited a few minutes to see if he would rise. When she heard his heavy morning footsteps, she relaxed against the chair at the kitchen table. She turned toward the laptop and logged onto Facebook, quickly scanning her friends' most recent updates. She relished the few moments of silence before the thunder of footsteps and the chatter of children.

Bootsie entered the kitchen, her nails tapping the ceramic tiles. She wagged her tail and sauntered over to the sliding glass doors, then looked expectantly at Jenny. "Okay, Boots, out you go." She opened the doors and the beagle rushed into the yard.

A few minutes later, she heard her husband's voice making the rounds to wake the children, his morning routine. "Time to get up, Chris and Chloe. Wake up, Callie and Cassie. Caleb... wake up, sleepyhead."

She logged off of Facebook, then pushed herself off the chair, her pregnant body heavy and cumbersome. She prepared Tom's lunch and packed it in his briefcase. She heard footsteps on the stairs, followed by two of her daughters, Chris and Chloe. Chloe was still in her pajamas, her curly red locks askew. Chris was already dressed, hair combed. She was only ten, but seemed so much older. Although Chris was almost an exact physical representation of Jenny at this age, her personality was Tom's, through and through. Bright, especially in math, a thinker. "Mom, I have a form to be signed."

"I'll do that in a minute, Chris."

Her eldest daughter sat at the kitchen table and leaned forward to speak to her younger sister. "Chloe, do you want cereal or toast?"

"Cereal."

Chris poured the cereal into a bowl.

Tom called from the top of the stairs. "Jen, where's my maroon tie?"

"Check the tie rack in the closet," she yelled back.

"It's not there."

"Then I don't know where it is."

"And I don't have any clean underwear either." She could hear him sighing from the top of the stairs.

"Sorry, Tom."

Her husband came down to the bottom step dressed in his terrycloth robe. He leaned his head toward the kitchen.

"Come on, Jen. Do I have to do everything in this house?" His tone was cutting and his words smacked her across the face. She frowned, turned away, but kept silent. Was this the same person who, just last night, told her to make sure she was taking it easy?

She heard him sigh again, then he said, "Look, I know you've had problems with this pregnancy and you need to rest, but what does it take to put a few pairs of underwear in the washer? I'll put them in the dryer when I return home."

Jenny cringed.   She fought the urge to respond with a nasty comment.   When she remained quiet, he asked, "Or perhaps I should ask my mother to come over?"

That did it.   She couldn't hold her tongue any longer. She turned to face him. "Yes, you should.   Then the house will be spotless, every piece of laundry will be washed, dried, ironed and folded and you'll always have meals prepared. In fact, perhaps you should have married your mother!"   She folded her arms and spun around to face her daughters.

"Come on, Jen," he said, as he rushed back up the stairs.

Tom's comment about his mother was a low blow. How dare he say that? He knew that she and Doris did not get along on the best of days. Jenny found herself wishing that her mom would return from Saskatchewan.   When Jenny needed help a few weeks ago, her mother had stayed with them the entire time, doing all the housework and never complaining.

"Mom, are you okay?" Chris was looking intensely at her.

Jenny nodded, but said nothing.

More loud pitter patter of steps and Cassie and Callie entered the kitchen dressed in identical pajamas. Caleb followed close behind, his teddy bear dragging on the floor, his footed pajamas making a padding sound.

A few minutes later, Tom came rushing down the stairs. He brushed against her when he picked up his briefcase beside the kitchen counter. Jenny kept silent. As he turned to leave, he stopped and faced her. She avoided eye contact. She knew what was coming: an immediate, less-than-heartfelt apology. It's the way he did things. A quick fix. But tonight, they'd need to talk, if she didn't give him the silent treatment. A few seconds passed by and she waited. Finally, he spoke, his voice hurried and rushed, without his usual gentle tone.

"Look, I'm sorry, Hon."   He leaned in, she supposed, to kiss the top of her head.   She kept her distance, but allowed him to make contact. He barely touched her, then turned and left.

When Jenny had woken up, she felt wonderful, with enough energy to clean the entire house. Now all she could think of was that she was a failure since she hadn't done the laundry in days. She forced herself to think lovingly of Tom, which was what Fr. Paul suggested the last time she confessed that she became angry with her husband. However, charity was *not* what she was feeling this morning.

"Mom, I need this paper signed." Chris held a paper in front of her face. "It's for a field trip to the Museum of Science and Technology."

Jenny scanned it, then signed it, and handed it back to her daughter.

"Come on, you guys, upstairs, get dressed. Chris, could you get me an outfit for your brother?"

Chris sighed, but did as she was told and in a few minutes returned with a pair of small jeans and a brown striped tee shirt.

"Don't like dat shirt, Mom," Caleb complained.

"Caleb, if you want to pick out your own clothes, do it before you come down." He fussed and whined, then became distracted with a toy while Jenny dressed him.

She finished making the lunches, then helped her daughters gather their backpacks. She quickly wrapped a cranberry muffin. Jenny locked the door. Her keys, cell phone and muffin were now in her purse.

At the bus stop, Chris tapped Jenny's shoulder. "Mom, you're not going to forget to meet us here today, right?"

"Of course not. I'll be here 15 minutes early." Jenny looked down the street and saw that the bus was about two blocks away. The hum of the bus and the smell of diesel exhaust grew closer.

"Thanks, Mom."

Jenny straightened and stared down at her daughter.

Chris's expression was serious and her frown was pronounced.

"Don't worry. I'll be here early."

Her daughter seemed to take a deep breath, then released it.   Cassie squealed. "Mom, that cloud looks like a boat!" Jenny glanced up at the whiteness against the blue sky.   One group of clouds did resemble a big fluffy ship. "You're right, Sweetie."

Caleb began to cry. "She hit me!"

"Come on, you guys. What's the matter?"

"He touched my Dora backpack," Chloe whined loudly.

Jenny sighed. "I'm sure your backpack will recuperate from the offensive touching." Chloe was frowning, her bright red curly hair seeming orange in the sun. Chloe was one of those extreme kids. Either she was very, very, happy or screaming her head off or crying her eyes out. But she was artistic and sensitive. "An irreplaceable eternal gift," as Blessed John Paul II, had said. *How could I have been upset when I realized I was pregnant with her?* The twins had just turned five months old. As much as Jenny greatly desired a large family, she had hoped and assumed that there would be at least a year before she became pregnant again. But she and Tom hadn't been keeping accurate natural family planning observations and within five months, she was pregnant with Chloe. The next two or three years were painfully difficult and there were times that she wanted to pull her hair out. But she survived. Of course, she couldn't imagine life without Chloe now, and was thankful that God had given them an unplanned gift.

The bus pulled up and the door opened. "Hello, Jenny," Frank Jenkins, the bus driver, said. He was a big, burly elderly man who treated her daughters like they were his own grandchildren. The girls always said that he reminded them of Santa Claus.

"Hello, Frank."

"It's a beautiful morning."

"It certainly is." Jenny handed Frank the small bag with a cranberry muffin.

"Thanks a bunch. I appreciate it, but you shouldn't worry about me."

"I'll be a little busy when the little one arrives and probably won't be baking at all."

"A little busy?" Frank laughed. Sometimes, Jenny half-expected him to say Ho, Ho, Ho, when he laughed like that.

"Have a good day and thanks again."

Jenny stepped back and the bus pulled away. She waved to the girls, who always sat on the right side so they could wave to her as they left.

Ever since Frank Jenkins had intervened for Chris last year when she was having problems with an older boy bullying her, Jenny couldn't think of enough ways to thank him. In small towns, people were always watching out for one another. It was one of the reasons Jenny loved living in Sutherland.

*   *   *

Today is the day, Denise thought with a smile. This morning, she had watched Jenny put her kids on the bus. If that girl knew what was in store for her today, she wouldn't be so happy. Denise was glad that she bought one of those hearing devices that allows you to eavesdrop on conversations across the street. Jenny had told the girls that she'd be waiting at the bus stop 15 minutes early today. With Jenny arriving well in advance of the bus, Denise would have ample time to grab her.

An hour beforehand, Denise filled the plastic cosmetic bag with vials of chloroform. She had ordered the drug from an online company which only sold to educational institutions. So she had asked her cousin if she could have a package sent to her at the high school where she worked.

Next, she placed some surgical gloves, hypodermic needles and vials filled with Ketamine (for keeping Jenny unconscious), Diazepam (to calm Jenny in case she was hysterical), and the Sleepaway euthanasia drug, all of which Denise had stolen from the animal hospital. Ketamine was easy to steal as it was left out frequently on afternoons Dr. Eastman performed surgery and wouldn't be missed because of spillage or miscalculation. However, the Diazepam and Sleepaway were more difficult, but Denise took the drugs when she was at the animal hospital alone for after hour treatments, making notes that she had spilled one or the other. By that time, Dr. Eastman was on maternity leave and no one ever questioned her about it.

Fritz, her terrier mix, followed her around as she went about her tasks. In the past few months, she anguished over what to do with him. He was, in fact, the only friend she really had and always offered her unconditional love. No human had ever done that. She didn't remember much about her mother, who died when she was four. Her father was an aloof alcoholic who drank his way through his grief, then to his grave when Denise was six years old. She spent time in foster care before moving in with her aunt, uncle and cousin, Anne, at the age of seven. Denise was hard-pressed to choose which was worse: foster care or her aunt and uncle who merely tolerated her presence.

She decided that she had no choice but to leave her beloved Fritz. She would make sure there was enough food, then eventually contact her cousin to take care of him. She crouched down to say goodbye to her best friend and patted him on the head.

Denise took the cosmetic bag and placed it in the front passenger seat of the car. One of the vials of Sleepaway was sticking out and she pushed it in and zipped up the bag.

A half hour before, Denise parked her Ford Taurus across the street at the bus stop. The rope sat in a circle on the floor of the back seat, the duct tape placed strategically in the middle and the dog leash lay on the seat. She took out her list and checked items off. Chloroform, other drugs, rope, tape, leash, full tank of gas for the ride. Surgical gloves were necessary so that when she was handling the leash, she wouldn't leave any fingerprints. As well, when she finished with her cigarettes, she made a point of throwing the butts in the trash can at the side of her house.

Tapping the steering wheel in a constant rhythm, she fidgeted with the radio dial, turning it to the country music station. It was now T minus 20. Denise got out of the car and stood next to the street sign. Her heart raced in rhythm and her hands started to shake. *Calm down, Dee. Take some deep breaths. You deserve this baby. She's already got five kids. You're just evening up the score.*

*   *   *

Caleb squirmed as he sat beside Jenny on the couch. She was reading, for the fifth time that afternoon, *Snowed in at Pokeweed Public School.* It didn't matter that it was sunny and warm; this was the book he always wanted to have read to him.

The phone rang and Jenny reached over Caleb to the end table for the cordless phone. "Hello?"

"Hey, Jen? How're you doing?" her friend, Ginger, asked.

"Fine. Just reading a story to Caleb."

"You mean that snowed in book again?"

"How'd you guess?"

"Our youngest is the same way with *Cat in the Hat.*"

"Go figure."

"By the way, tell your husband that the Professor and Mary Ann are doing fine."

Jenny chuckled. Tom was always teasing Ginger about her name, occasionally asking her how the Skipper and Gilligan were doing. The joke was getting old, but Tom continued. He was such a goofy guy sometimes. Jenny's attitude had softened since this morning. She was tempted to share with her friend the fight that she and her husband had this morning, but she decided not to mention it.

They chatted for a few moments and said good bye. For

years, Jenny and Tom had prayed for Ginger and her husband, Gary. The couple had tried for seven years to get pregnant, eventually resorting to fertility drugs. When they didn't become pregnant, they applied to adopt a baby girl from China. It was expensive, but within four years, they had brought home two adorable black-haired girls named Hope and Faith and were scheduled to pick up their third daughter in three months.

Jenny glanced at her watch. It was 20 minutes before the bus would arrive, but she had promised Chris that she would be at the bus stop early. It only took four minutes to walk there, although sometimes it was a minute or so longer if Caleb decided to dawdle.

*   *   *

Tom Callahan sat in front of his computer in his office. For the last two hours, he had been working on Greg Wilkins' income and expense report for the Wilkins' upcoming divorce trial. Many of his clients were going through divorces right now, and it wasn't unusual for someone to request accounting documents for support and custody hearings. He shook his head. It bothered him that he was profiting from a couple's marital breakup, especially since he didn't believe in divorce. What he had to endure during his parents' split three years ago was painful, and he was an adult. He couldn't imagine going through that as a child.

He relaxed in his chair and stared blankly at the monitor. His stomach growled. His day had been so busy; he hadn't had time to eat. Reaching into his briefcase, he pulled out his lunch box. Inside were a turkey sandwich, bottled water, an orange and two homemade cranberry muffins. He took a few bites of the sandwich, then wiped his mouth with the napkin. As he did so, he saw there was some writing on it. Jen must have written it before he spoke to her this morning. *I love you.* He closed his eyes as he recalled his caustic words to her earlier today. He grinned as he thought of her response about marrying his mother.

His smile faded. He hated himself when he spoke to her that way. Tom wasn't a morning person, just the opposite, and he was under a lot of stress trying to prepare for a meeting with an influential prospective client. On top of that, Caleb had crawled into bed with them during the night. Despite the fact that his son always wore a pull up to bed, Tom woke up to wet sheets. After Tom had taken his shower, he had gone to find a clean pair of underwear in his drawer and there wasn't one to be found. That he had been annoyed would probably be an understatement. But it was no excuse for his behavior.

It didn't normally bother him when Jen didn't keep up with the laundry or housework, especially during pregnancy. Sometimes when he came home from work, Jen would be sitting on the floor playing Barbies with the girls or reading a book to Caleb or some other kid-centered activity. It was precisely that type of behavior which made Tom fall more in love with her.

Of course, with the most recent problems with this pregnancy as well as the previous miscarriages, he knew that she needed to stay off her feet. With the way he spoke to her this morning, chances are, she had already done the laundry. But she probably didn't have dinner planned yet. He picked up the phone and dialed. He wanted to apologize. To make it up to her, he would splurge and get some take out food so she wouldn't have to cook supper this evening.

*   *   *

As Jenny was closing the door to leave, the phone rang. She hesitated, trying to decide whether she ought to answer it. With call display and voice mail, she could easily call the person back when she returned home from the bus stop. Jenny also kept her cell phone in her purse. Since only a few select people had her cell number, if it was an urgent matter, they would call her cell.

She pulled the door shut. Jenny was determined not to be late today, especially after she promised Chris that she would be there.

* * *

Tom hung up the phone and was in the process of dialing his wife's cell when his secretary approached his desk.

"Mr. Waverly asked to see you in his office."

"Sure thing," he said, as he replaced the receiver.

* * *

Jenny and her son began the short jaunt up the street to the bus stop. Caleb, at three years of age, was not walking as fast as she'd like, but it was still about ten minutes before the bus would arrive.

Her mom had offered to pick up the kids from the bus stop next week, as well as perform the household duties when Jenny was closer to delivery. Jenny understood why her mom wanted to be with her ailing sister in Saskatchewan, but she secretly wished that she would return sooner.

She thought back to Tom's question about his mom coming over and helping her out at home. He wasn't serious — just angry — which was why he suggested it. But it annoyed her when Tom mentioned his mother in an argument.

Since the separation, then divorce, of Tom's parents three years ago, Doris had become increasingly belligerent. Jenny tried to be sensitive to her mother-in-law's emotional highs and lows. But on a bad day, Jenny was almost always on the receiving end of any criticisms and cross comments. Doris had always been critical of Jenny's laissez-faire attitude towards housekeeping, but generally speaking, before the divorce, her mother-in-law kept her comments to herself. Since the break up, however, that had changed.

As she approached the bus stop, Jenny noticed a woman there. *That's odd. My girls are the only ones who get off at this stop. I wonder why she's standing there.* Immediately, she became uneasy and looked away. *Stop it, Jen. This is Sutherland, a quiet neighborhood with virtually no crime rate.*

She continued walking until she could see her face. The woman was smoking and staring into the distance. As usual, the neighborhood was deserted until the kids returned home from school.

The lady looked familiar. She was tall, although slightly overweight. Jenny glanced at her middle and realized that the woman was wearing a maternity top. When Jenny moved closer, the woman finally made eye contact. "Hello, Jenny. How are you?"

"Uh. . .I'm fine. Are you waiting for somebody?"

"I'm waiting for you." The woman dropped the cigarette on the ground and stamped it out.

"Me? Do I know you?"

"Uh-huh. I work at the Sutherland Veterinary Hospital."

"Oh, right."

"How's Bootsie doing?"

"She's fine, uh. . ."

"Denise."

"Right, Denise."

"I remembered that you were expecting pretty soon, right?"

"Yes. You too?"

"Uh. . .yes, me too."

"When are you due?"

"Around the same time as you."

"Oh?" Jenny's large round stomach looked like it was a basketball compared to this woman, who appeared to be six months pregnant at most. *She must be having a small baby.*

"Well, you know," Denise continued, "my cousin's got these maternity and baby clothes and they're all high end stuff and I remembered seeing you and wondered if you might like them."

"That's nice of you, but don't you need them?"

"I've already taken a bunch and these are the ones I won't use. Come over here. I've got them right here in my car."

Jenny thought the woman was a bit strange, and again, she felt uneasy, but she wanted to be polite. After all, she knew her from the vet's office and she was pregnant. If you can't trust a pregnant woman, who *can* you trust? "I guess it can't hurt to take a look, but I'm almost ready to deliver and won't be needing any maternity clothes." Denise walked quickly to a car parked close by, Jenny and Caleb following behind. She could see the woman opening up the back door and leaning in. She stepped back. "Right in there."

Jenny lowered her head to peer inside. She couldn't see clothes anywhere. All of a sudden, she felt something smashed against her face and nose. Breathing in a vaguely sweet scent, she jerked her head from side to side. She opened her mouth to cry out and inadvertently inhaled. She tried to move her arms, but she immediately went limp.

Four

I wish that kid would shut up. Denise wouldn't have time to tie Jenny up right now, but she used enough chloroform to keep her asleep on the back seat for at least twenty minutes. Denise turned toward the crying toddler. Perhaps she ought to give him a whiff of the chloroform. She reconsidered.

"It's okay, little fellow. Your sisters will be here in a few minutes." She tried to speak calmly, despite the wretched screaming. Denise quickly put the surgical gloves on, slipped the dog leash over the squirming boy, tightening it around his small chest. He wiggled out of it and she grabbed him. "Stop it right now!" She smacked his hand. Surprised, his eyes widened and he froze long enough for her to put the leash around him. He pulled the strap out of her hands, but she quickly whipped it away and roughly tethered it to the street sign. She yanked on it to make sure it was secure. He continued to wail.

She slipped in behind the wheel of the car and sped off. As she was driving away, Denise took a quick glance in the rearview mirror, and she could see that the kid's mouth was wide open as he screamed. She now relished the quiet hum of the car's motor.

Her hands were trembling and her heart was racing. She took the surgical gloves off and reached into her purse for her cigarettes. Denise took one out and lit it, inhaled and immediately calmed down. She had finally done it. Jenny Callahan was unconscious and in the back seat of her car. Maybe if she was traumatized enough, she'd give birth right away and Denise wouldn't have to wait long for the baby to be born. Soon she would have a baby to call her own.

"Mrs. Kramer, you have scarred fallopian tubes."
"I have what?"

"Scarred fallopian tubes, probably as the result of pelvic inflammatory disease."

"I have a disease?"

"Well, what it means is that sometime over the past 15 or 20 years, you contracted a sexually transmitted infection and it was never treated."

"But I want to have a baby."

"Since the fallopian tubes are what carry the egg to the womb, and since yours are scarred, the only way that will happen, Mrs. Kramer, is through in-vitro fertilization or adoption."

Ding, ding, ding. The seat belt alarm was now ringing and she realized that it had become detached behind her. She never wore one anyway — it was too uncomfortable — but she usually kept it connected and behind her.

Denise drove for a few minutes on the rural roads, then she pulled over. She quickly buckled the seat belt to stop the alarm, then opened the back door. For just having been kidnapped, Jenny looked surprisingly peaceful. She taped the unconscious woman's mouth. Bringing her two limp hands together, Denise tied them firmly with a piece of rope, using a Boy Scout knot which Lou had taught her when they went camping years ago.

The sound of an unfamiliar cell phone ringing made her jump. Jenny's purse sat on the floor. She rummaged around until she found the phone. After six rings, it went silent. Denise stared at it as it sat in the palm of her gloved hand. With new technology, she wondered whether a cell phone could be easily found, regardless of whether the power was on or off. If that was the case, she wouldn't want it anywhere near her. She tossed it as far as she could off the side of the road.

Turning her attention again to the pregnant woman, Denise wrapped Jenny's feet with duct tape, paying special attention to keeping it taut but not too tight. She stared at

Jenny's large abdomen and imagined the baby inside. Resisting the urge to touch it, she retrieved the hypodermic needle, filled it with Ketamine, and injected the woman's thigh. Denise knew the importance of giving Jenny a low enough dosage to keep her unconscious; she had to be careful because a Ketamine overdose could harm the baby. "There, that should keep you out for a few hours." Denise couldn't risk Jenny wakening until she reached the cottage and had the girl chained to the bed.

She slammed the door, returned to the driver's seat and drove away. The next stop was the cottage 40 kilometers away. It was the ideal place to keep her because it was a half a kilometer from any other cottage in the area, which would be important in case Jenny woke up and screamed. The only ones who might hear her would be the wild animals.

For the last two weeks, she had stocked the cottage with food, wood and extra supplies. She had visited one of those home birth websites to get a list of materials needed for birth. She figured it wouldn't be difficult to deliver a baby, especially one whose mother had given birth many times before. A doctor on TV had said that women have been giving birth for thousands of years without intervention. Once the baby was born, Denise would use the Sleepaway to kill Jenny and be on her way. After all, she wasn't a monster who wanted Jenny to suffer needlessly. A good dose of the euthanasia drug would make Jenny fall asleep and never wake up.

Everything was planned perfectly, right down to the clothes her new baby would wear.

Five

As the school bus turned the corner, Christine Callahan craned her neck to see out the front window. There was no sign of her mom, but it appeared as if someone had tied a dog...no, it wasn't a dog. Chris let out a scream when she saw who was tied to the street sign. Her brother was sitting on the ground and crying.

"What's the matter, Christine?" Mr. Jenkins asked.

"Caleb!" she yelled again.

The bus stopped and the driver opened the doors. Chris rushed down the steps and onto the sidewalk. "Hey, Sport, are you okay? Where's Mommy?" Her brother's tears ran down his face like little dirt roads and he was hiccupping from crying so hard.

"Mommy... gone."

Chris felt her knees buckle and she drew in a breath. "What do you mean Mommy's gone?"

"Is everything all right, Christine?" asked Mr. Jenkins, as he stepped down from the bus.

"No, Mr. Jenkins, it's not! Something's...happened to...!" Chris tried to say it without stammering but she couldn't get the rest of the sentence out. Finally, she said, "My mom, Mr. Jenkins."

"Okay, Christine. Calm down."

He leaned down to talk to Caleb.

"Where's your mommy?"

"Mommy gone. She gone, Chrissie. Mommy gone. Don't like lady."

"What lady, Caleb?"

"Don't like dat lady, Chrissie. Took Mommy."

"Oh no!"

"Where's Mommy? Where's Mommy?" Callie began to cry. She and her other sisters were still on the bus, standing at the top of the steps. Chris reached up and helped them down the steps.

"Chris, stay here with your brother and sisters. I'm going to get my cell phone from the bus." Before the end of a minute, Mr. Jenkins was back and dialing his cell phone.

"Yes, this is Frank Jenkins. I'm a school bus driver for the St. Bartholomew's route. I stopped to let four sisters off at their bus stop and not only was their mother not there, but their little brother was tied to the street sign. We need a police officer here immediately." Mr. Jenkins listened for a moment and said, "Okay. I'll remain on the line until the officers arrive." He looked down at her. "The police will be here shortly, Chris."

The seven remaining children on the school bus were now standing at the top of the steps watching the scene below.

"I'll wait with you until they arrive."

"You need to call my dad, Mr. Jenkins. You need to call him now, please!"

Mr. Jenkins lifted his eyes to the sky and listened. Very faint police sirens became louder by the second. He then spoke into his phone. "I'm going to hang up because I need to call the children's father, okay?" He clapped the phone shut.

"Do you know your dad's phone number at work?"

Chris nodded and gave it to him.

"That's good, Christine, area code and all. You're so smart." She winced at being called smart now. She just wanted her mom to come home and to know that she was safe.

He dialed the number and Chris prayed that her dad would answer the phone.

"Mr. Callahan, my name is Frank Jenkins. I'm the..." He smiled awkwardly at Chris. "Oh, I'm fine, Mr. Callahan."

"Please, let me talk to my dad," Chris pleaded, taking the phone from him.

"Daddy, Mommy's gone." She began to whimper.

"Calm down, honey. What do you mean Mommy's gone?"

"We just got to the bus stop and Caleb's tied to the sign and Mommy's not here." She couldn't get the words out fast enough.

"Oh my God," her dad said, in a whisper. For a second, he was silent. Then he said, "Don't worry, I'll be there as soon as possible. Let me talk to Mr. Jenkins."

"Okay, Daddy." She handed the phone to Mr. Jenkins, but his end of the conversation became background noise as she gathered her four younger siblings in front of her. Her sisters were crying.

"Yes," said the bus driver. "I'll wait here until the police arrive then I have to drive the other children home. Yes. Yes. Okay."

As he flipped his phone closed, he looked down at Christine. "Your dad's gonna call your grandmom to come and stay with you, but he said he'll be home very soon."

Chris bit down on her lip to keep herself from crying.

Police sirens could be heard close by and Chris looked up at Mr. Jenkins. She was scared for her mom. But she was the oldest and she knew she had to be calm, or else her younger brother and sisters would get more upset. She tried to take deep even breaths, but it was becoming difficult to breathe at all.

Her younger sisters moved closer to her and she pulled Caleb in front of her. "Shhh." She crouched down. Chloe was starting to cry louder than Caleb. "It's all right, Chloe."

The sirens wailed as a police car pulled up. Two policemen got out. One was tall and skinny with blond hair and one was shorter and chunky with dark hair. Christine watched as they approached Mr. Jenkins. She couldn't hear everything they said. Finally, the shorter cop leaned down and spoke in a calm voice.

"Hi. You're Christine?"

"Uh-huh," she said, pulling Caleb closer to her.

"My name is Constable Bob. I'm a police officer."

Chris knew that he was trying to be nice, but she didn't like it when adults treated her like she was a baby.

"Mommy gone," said Caleb.

"I see," said the cop. "What's your name, little fellow?"

"Kay-ulb," he said, drawing out the "ulb" part of it so he couldn't understand.

"His name's Caleb, sir," Chris answered.

"Caleb. Good biblical name. My oldest son's name is Jeremiah. But he's big now, at high school."

Chris nodded, but at the same time, she wanted to scream. *My mom's out there and somebody took her and she needs help ....why are you asking all these questions?* "When are you going to find my mom?"

"Christine, your mom was expecting a baby?"

She nodded. "She's going to have the baby next week."

Caleb began to scream. "Want Mommy, Chrissie!"

The shorter police officer whispered to the taller officer, then he pointed to a woman in a police uniform. "Christine, that nice lady is going to take you home. Your grandmother will be there to watch over you, okay?"

Chris tried to say yes, but instead she bit her lip as she listened to Caleb yell and her sisters crying. Her own sob crept up the back of her throat. What if her mom was hurt...or worse?

"Now, go along with this nice policewoman. She will walk you home."

Once home, the lady police officer tried the front door, but it was locked.

"Mom keeps a key behind the mailbox in an envelope," Chris offered.

The lady retrieved the key and opened the door.

Inside, Bootsie was barking at the lady but wagging her tail at the children. "You guys go into the living room and watch TV," Chris offered. They remained at her side, but she urged them to go. The three girls and Caleb hurried into the living room.

The lady stooped down and patted Bootsie on the head.

"Oh, there you are," she heard Grandmom's voice behind them as she was coming through the front doorway. Chris was glad that her grandmother lived close by. The two women spoke for a moment, then the lady police officer left. Grandmom crouched down in front of Chris.

"Mommy's missing. Caleb..."

"Chris," Grandmom said calmly, "everything's going to be fine, just fine. The nice police officers are going to do all they can to find your mom."

Chris didn't want to hear that right now. What she wanted was to see her mom come through the door and say that it was all a mistake, that she really was fine. But that wasn't going to happen. Her mom wasn't fine; she was gone and nobody knew where she was.

*   *   *

Ontario Provincial Police Sergeant Kathy Romano was in the middle of a late lunch in Kanata, a suburb of Ottawa, when her BlackBerry rang. She answered it, spoke for a few moments, then hung up and took the last bite of her club sandwich.

At first, she thought she misheard the word "kidnapping" and asked her supervisor to repeat it. Violent crime in Sutherland was rare.

She apologized to her sister for having to cut their lunch short. As Area Crime Sergeant in charge of the Local OPP Detachment, Kathy would be driving back to Sutherland to oversee an investigation involving a pregnant mother of five who had been abducted from a school bus stop. A detective inspector was already on his way from the Benchmark Crimes Division in Orillia as case manager, but Kathy would be overseeing the boots-on-the-ground response.

Her orders were to immediately proceed to the scene of the crime and direct the investigation.

Once in her car, she turned on the siren, then switched on the flashing light that sat on her dashboard. Having the portable light and siren made it possible for her to travel to the scene in half the time. She especially appreciated the siren and light when she was driving in her unmarked car on major highways and a car passed her with lightning speed. She wasn't in the habit of giving speeding tickets, but she made an exception for heavy footers.

On her way to Sutherland, she considered the crime. Sutherland was only ten minutes from Pakenham, her home town. The last time Sutherland had seen any sort of crime was when a divorced non-custodial father took off with his kids five years ago.

The first question she always asked in a situation like this was "Why?" Motive was not usually obvious, although the abduction of a pregnant woman most often indicated that someone wanted the baby. Generally speaking, the suspect was a woman, usually infertile and most often unstable. She also knew from experience these women generally don't want a ransom and frequently kill their victims in the first hour or so. She found herself hoping that this suspect wouldn't be one of those.

Unless, of course, the suspect was the victim's husband.

Victimology was the other important key in a case like this. Who was Jenny Callahan? Had she known the person who abducted her? Statistically, there was usually some kind of connection between the perpetrator and the victim. But in small towns, just about everybody knows everybody else and it was easy to find a connection between most people.

Activating her OnStar, she dialed her husband's home office number. He answered on the second ring.

"Hey. I'm not going to be home tonight. Kidnapping. I'll probably be staying at the station." Even though Kathy lived ten minutes away from Sutherland, in the small town of Braeside, she knew it would be best to stay at the station for the duration of the investigation.

"Kidnapping?"

"Yes. Which means I'll be bunking out there for a while. Let Danny know I love him."

"Sure thing."

She hung up and pictured her husband telling their 14-year-old son, "Your mom said to tell you she loves you." His amused, but at the same time annoyed, expression would be priceless. Of course, she always avoided public displays of affection, but when Danny was home, with none of his peers watching, he was fair game for a quick hug and kiss.

Running her fingers through her shoulder length dark hair, she found herself thankful that she had followed her hairdresser's advice and got it cut short. Especially now, she needed an easy-to-maintain style.

She made it to the scene in 18 minutes and quickly got out of her car. A forensic identification unit consisting of three technicians was already collecting evidence. Four police constables were interviewing people in the now growing crowd. Three news vans were already on the scene.

She approached Constables Anderson and Preston, whom everyone at the detachment called Laurel and Hardy. It wasn't a fair term because Bob Preston, the shorter and stockier of the two really looked nothing like Oliver Hardy. They stepped away from the people.

"What have we got?" she asked them.

Bob Preston spoke first. "Victim's name is Jenny Callahan. She's nine months pregnant and usually picks her kids up at this bus stop. When the bus arrived, Mrs. Callahan's son was found tethered to the sign."

"How old's the boy, Bob?"

"Three."

"Then I suppose he couldn't give you a description?"

"We didn't interview him. He was taken back to his home down the street. News vans are already starting to gather here and in front of the house." Constable Preston pointed to an area a few blocks away.

"Yeah, the kid started crying. His sisters — Mrs. Callahan's daughters — were upset. We figured that you could interview them all at their home," Constable Jeff Anderson, the taller man, offered.

"Very well." Kathy walked toward one of the crime scene investigators, a short middle-aged woman, dusting the sign pole for prints. "Anything, Em?"

"Not much. Lots of prints on the pole, nothing on the leash."

"Thanks."

She approached a young male crime scene tech who was taking photographs. "Anything here, Ben?"

He looked up from the camera. "One cigarette butt." The man turned and began taking more photographs.

Kathy decided that it was time to head to the Callahan residence. As she walked toward her car, she turned and motioned for Constable Anderson to accompany her. Approaching Constable Preston, she asked, "Has anyone questioned the neighbors?"

"We've started, but it looks like most of the houses near the bus stop are unoccupied during the day."

"Have constables go door to door asking questions and again when people start to arrive home. Someone must've seen something."

"All right."

"What's the address of the Callahan residence?"

Constable Preston looked down at his notepad. "2407 Hudson Lane...one block down and one block over."

"Thanks."

Constable Anderson got into the passenger seat of Kathy's car. She slipped into the driver's seat, punched the address in her GPS and began to drive.

"Turn next left at Smithson Street," the GPS's male voice commanded.

"Jeff, I'm going to assign you to remain at the residence. In a situation like this, we need police presence at the house.

I already ordered that all incoming phone calls will be traced from the OPP station."

* * *

Tom Callahan waited at the exit of the parking lot for his building in downtown Ottawa. He nervously tapped the wheel. Even without traffic, the ride home would take at least an hour. His mother was with the kids, so for that he was thankful. *This has to be some terrible mistake.* He dialed Jen's cell phone again.

Six

The Callahan residence was a small, albeit quaint, two story Cape Cod with light green shutters, a tiny porch and purple and yellow flowers in front of the bay window. Knowing that the victim and her husband had five children and one on the way, Kathy couldn't imagine raising that many children in this small home.

Kathy and Constable Anderson stepped onto the narrow porch. Before they had a chance to knock, the door swung open. A tall, older woman with graying auburn hair, wearing dress pants and a short-sleeved pink sweater stood before them. Immediately, Kathy was struck by the overpowering scent of some sort of sweet-musky perfume.

The older woman wore no hint of a smile and her stature rivaled that of a mannequin. Kathy, at five feet ten inches tall, often found herself slouching, so she immediately straightened. She had been told by Bob Preston that Jenny Callahan's mother-in-law would be staying with the children until the victim's husband arrived home.

Kathy held out her badge. "Mrs. Callahan?"

"Yes?" The woman forced a smile.

"I'm Sergeant Romano with the Ontario Provincial Police. This is Constable Anderson. May we come in?"

"My son isn't home yet. But, yes, please do come in," she said as she opened the door wider and allowed them to come inside. The television was blaring in what Kathy figured was a living room to the right.

The foyer was cramped and Constable Anderson was forced to stand on the bottom step of the staircase leading upstairs as Mrs. Callahan closed the door. A short table beside the door held today's mail.

Kathy leaned her head inside the doorway to the small living room, and observed a group of mostly red-haired children sitting quietly on the floor watching a television show that featured a black man dressed in an orange suit. A brown-haired girl glanced back and Kathy smiled at her. The girl didn't return the gesture. Instead, she looked away, then stared off in the distance.

Kathy observed a large kitchen area at the end of the hallway. She faced Mrs. Callahan. "This officer is going to remain at the house for the next several hours, until he's off shift."

Mrs. Callahan brought her hand forward and Constable Anderson shook it. "Nice to meet you, Constable."

"May I speak with your grandson?" Kathy asked, looking at her notepad, "Caleb?"

"Yes, certainly, although I don't know how much he can tell you, Sergeant. He's just a baby."

"Thank you."

The two officers walked through the living room on their way to the kitchen, then Mrs. Callahan stopped and leaned down. "Caleb, this nice lady wants to talk to you." She took hold of the boy's hand and led him to the kitchen, which was a large country-style kitchen three times the size of the living room. Dishes were piled on the table and counters as well as the sink and three baskets of laundry lined the far wall. The front of the refrigerator was a hodge podge of small photos, kids' artwork and various magnets. Kathy turned around to see the older girl standing behind her.

* * *

Chris followed the group into the kitchen. There were two people, a cop and a tall lady. The lady wasn't wearing a uniform, just some slacks and a nice shirt, but she was probably a cop, an important one because Chris heard her say she was "in charge." The lady turned and spoke to her. "Hi, there."

"Hi."

"What's your name?"

"Christine."

"Hi, Christine. My name is Kathy. You can return to the television if you'd like."

"I need to be with my brother, ma'am," Chris said.

"That's not necessary," the lady cop said.

"My little brother needs me."

"All right."

The lady cop stood at the kitchen table. Chris picked Caleb up. She placed him in his booster seat then took the seat beside him. Grandmom remained standing, eyeing the table, her eyebrows raised. Chris groaned inwardly when she had realized that the lunch dishes hadn't yet been cleared and washed. It looked like someone (probably Caleb) hadn't finished a grilled cheese sandwich. His glass of milk was half-full and probably warm by now.

The tall lady cop crouched down to speak to Caleb. "Now, Caleb..." She was interrupted by Grandmom who quickly cleared the table, then returned a few seconds later to wipe the surface.

"Caleb, my name is Kathy and I'm trying to find out who took your mom. Can you tell me what the lady looked like, the one who took your mommy?"

"She big and smelled bad."

"Smelled bad how?"

"Like smoke."

"Did you see what color hair she had, honey?"

"Uh...brown."

"Was it short hair or long?"

"Short, like you."

"Do you remember what she was wearing?"

"Dunno."

"Can you tell me what happened?"

"Pushed mommy into car. Mommy fell in car. Tied me. No like her."

"Do you remember what color the car was?"

"Dunno."

"What was your mom wearing?"

"Dunno."

"Caleb, did the lady who took your mom say anything to her?"

"Dunno."

"What are you going to do to find my mom?" Christine stood and stared at the lady.

"Everything we possibly can, honey."

Chris liked the lady cop, but she didn't like being called "Honey" unless by her parents. Honey is what grown ups called little kids and, at ten years old, she was not a little kid.

Turning to Grandmom, the lady cop asked, "Do you have a recent photo of the family or of Mrs. Callahan that we could use?"

Grandmom reached for her purse and pulled out a small photo. "Here," she said. "It was taken last year before Jenny became pregnant."

"Mrs. Callahan, thank you. I'd better return to the scene. I'll be back shortly when your son arrives home."

Her grandmother and the lady cop walked toward the living room and the front door. They were saying something that Chris couldn't hear, but she guessed. The lady cop was probably telling Grandmom to keep the kids calm. Chris lifted Caleb out of his booster seat and he ran into the living room.

Chris watched him plop down in front of the TV with her three younger sisters. Cassie looked up at her. Her sister had tears in her eyes and rushed over to her. The little girl began to cry. "Mommy's gonna be all right, isn't she, Chrissie?"

Chris bit down on her lip and tried hard not to cry, but she had this horrible feeling in the pit of her stomach. A sob crept up the back of her throat and there was nothing she could do to stop it. She began to cry and, all of a sudden, Grandmom was hugging them, comforting them and holding them close.

* * *

Sitting in her car, Kathy smiled as she thought of little Caleb Callahan. This bright toddler gave her a good starting description. She knew that the woman who took Jenny Callahan had short, brown hair and was likely a smoker. From her experience, she suspected that the woman was infertile and wanted a baby. That the perpetrator left the toddler alive at the scene gave Kathy hope that Jenny was still alive.

Kathy studied the portrait of the Callahan family, which Jenny's mother-in-law had just given to her. The children were all dressed in the same or similar outfits. *Jenny's a girl after my own heart.*

Kathy stared down at the picture and into the faces of Tom and Jenny. There was no mistaking the happiness in both their expressions. It was unusual these days to see a family with more than three children. Despite the expressions, could there be more to the story than the happy family this photo illustrated? Her intuition told her that this was a stranger abduction. However, she would continue to study the evidence to see where it would lead.

Seven

Tom Callahan raced home via the Queensway highway. He hated the fact that it was going to take him another 15 minutes, no matter how fast he drove. He pressed redial on his cell phone. He had called Jen's cell phone constantly since he found out that she was missing. Each time he pressed redial, his hope evaporated when she didn't pick up.

"Calm down," he said to himself, trying to take deep breaths. "This has got to be a mistake. There must be some explanation." He tried to reassure himself, but the sinking feeling in his stomach became more intense with every passing moment.

Tom's breathing became shallow, his heart continued to pound. "Jesus, Mary and Joseph, she's pregnant. God, please, please help her. Blessed Mother, wherever she is right now, please, please protect her."

This morning, all he could focus on was the business meeting with his new client, Caleb's wetting the bed and the lack of clean underwear. In the grand scheme of things, those were such trivial and stupid reasons to be in a bad mood. But like it or not, that had been his state of mind when he said goodbye to Jen this morning.

"Please God, let Jen be safe. Let her come home so I can tell her what she means to me...."

Thirteen years earlier

Tom focused on the Calculus problem on his desk. He kept one ear open in case Mrs. Needham called on him to answer a history question. Finishing the last equation, Tom slipped his notebook and calculator into his math binder and pulled out his history book.

It was only the second week of his last year of high school, but Tom already had several hours of homework each night. That, combined with football practice every afternoon, meant that he had practically no free time. And last night, he had made the mistake of turning on the television at 7:00 to watch a rerun of Gilligan's Island, and then promptly fell asleep without finishing his math homework. Not that Calculus was difficult; it came easily to Tom, who would be applying to Queens University two hours away. With his solid high grades, he was hopeful that he'd get an offer and perhaps a football scholarship to his father's alma mater.

He heard a slamming noise to the right of him and glanced across the aisle and one seat back to see Jenny Hathaway lean down to pick up her history book. Jeff Anderson's snickering from the seat behind her suggested that he was up to no good again. Tom couldn't help but feel sorry for Jenny. He had heard that her father had recently died and that she had moved to Sutherland from Saskatchewan. Tough break for someone to be in a new school during their last year of high school. He couldn't see Jenny's face now, but he thought he could hear her sighing.

"Psst, Tom?"

Tom groaned as he felt the ruler jabbing his back.

"Got an extra pencil?" he heard Naomi whisper.

He turned around and saw that she had her eyebrows raised, waiting for him to answer.

"No, I don't have an extra pencil," he whispered back. For a minute, he thought he could see her eyes flutter. He shook his head, then faced the front. Tom realized that he was not the best looking guy in his class, but he was first string football and that supposedly made him desirable to all the superficial girls who just wanted to be on the arm of a football player. And if one more girl told him that he looked like a young Ron Howard, he would scream.

The bell rang and Tom slipped his books inside his bag and stood up. Mrs. Needham opened the door, stood in the hallway and began talking with someone from the main office.

Snickering and laughing coming from Jeff's general vicinity made Tom roll his eyes. Jeff was pointing at Jenny, who stood still and silent, her lips pursed, her face flushed, her eyes beginning to tear. What did that jerk do to her to make her upset? Students walked by her, no one making any attempt her to assist her. Jeff and his friends continued walking to the door, laughing and pointing at Jenny.

Tom inched his way toward the young girl, her head now down and her hands covering her face. Her feet were fixed to the ground. Kids continued to whisper and laugh, pointing at her and walking around her.

Looking for Mrs. Needham, Tom could see that she was still standing in the hallway, her back to the classroom, oblivious to the commotion.

Why was Jenny so upset?

Another student bumped into Tom and whispered, "She's on the rag."

Tom scowled at him, then tilted his head to look at the back of her pants and cringed. He hesitated, awkwardly wondering what, if anything, he ought to do.

After a few seconds, Tom slipped his football sweater off and stood in front of her. "Jenny?" She stood still, but he could see now that she was shaking. Reaching out to touch her shoulder, he whispered, "Jenny?" When there was no response, he slipped his sweater around her waist and tied the sleeves. As he stood in front of her, she slowly brought her gaze up to his and stared at him with a confused, sad expression that reminded Tom of a cat who had just been hit by a car and who didn't know whether to trust the person helping him. "Jenny, I'm Tom. Come on, I'll take you to the girls' room." At first, she shook her head, resisting him. But he gently held on to her arm, urging her to come with him and pulling her across the hall to the girls' bathroom.

"Here," he said. "I'll wait for you, if you want." She nodded so slightly that Tom wasn't sure it was even an answer. She walked away and into the bathroom.

Several girls emerged from the washroom, whispering and snickering to one another. He heard one of the girls say "Jenny." People could be so cruel, he thought, then the bell rang for the next class to begin. As the teacher walked into her classroom, she called, "Mr. Callahan, shouldn't you be in your next class?" He wanted to say "Shouldn't you be helping your students?" Instead he replied, "I'm helping Jenny Hathaway. She's not feeling well. We'll both go to the office when I know she's all right." Mrs. Needham nodded and returned to her classroom and closed the door.

If another teacher walked by, he'd probably get a detention slip for being in the hallway, but hopefully, the teacher would allow him to explain why he was standing outside the girls' bathroom.

Several long moments crept by and, finally, Jenny emerged from the bathroom, her eyes avoiding his, his sweater still draped around her waist.

"You all right?" he asked her.

She gulped, then quietly said, "I...hope I didn't...ruin your sweater."

"Nah, don't worry about that. Hey, we better get to the office and let them know what's going on." When Tom glanced at Jenny's face, her eyes widened, her head lowered.

"Don't worry. I won't tell them exactly what happened. I'll just say you're not feeling well."

She sighed, but kept her gaze downward.

"Are you okay?" he asked again.

She quickly shook her head.

"Wanna go home?"

She nodded.

"All right. We'll just make a quick stop at the office to let them know I'm taking you home."

"You're taking me home?" she asked, her eyes now staring at his.

"Sure. My mom lets me take the spare car to school every day. I can drive you home and come back."

"Really?"

"Sure. Come on."

The two of them stopped by the office and Tom explained that he was taking Jenny home because she wasn't feeling well. Then they walked to the car.

Tom opened the door and saw her hesitate.

"I don't want to mess up your mom's car."

"Right."

He walked around to the trunk, removed the emergency blanket and put it on the car seat. He felt badly even doing that, but he needed to have a backup, just in case. If his mom saw the stain, she would question it and perhaps get angry.

In the car, Jenny said little and Tom, now feeling more awkward, asked, "Uh...where do you live?"

"On Donner Street, just off Kirkman Road." The tone of her voice was timid and quiet and Tom had to strain to hear the second street's name.

"Kirkman, you said?"

"Uh-huh."

From Tom's estimate, it would take at least ten minutes to arrive at Jenny's house. At the stop light, he looked at Jenny, who was just glancing away from him. He hadn't really noticed before, but Jenny was a very pretty girl, not a lot of make up like the stuck up girls who just wanted to date him because he was on the football team. In fact, with her long straight brown hair, Jenny reminded Tom of those wholesome girls from the 70's.

As he drove off Kirkman to Donner Street, Jenny spoke. "My house is the third one on the right, the yellow one with the white picket fence." Tom pulled to a stop in front of her house and expected her to jump right out. Instead, she waited. Again, Tom felt awkward in the ensuing silence. She finally turned to him and said, "Thank you...you probably told me, but I don't remember your name."

"Tom...Tom Callahan."

"Thank you, Tom."

"Don't mention it."

"Why..."

"Why what?"

"Why did you help me?"

Tom let out a quiet chuckle. "I've got three sisters. A few weeks ago, the same thing happened to my sister, Patty, at the mall and she made me walk behind her all the way out to the parking lot."

"I suppose that's the reason some people call it the curse, but my mom always called it 'tears of a disappointed uterus' since she wasn't able to have children naturally." Jenny paused, then continued. "I hope it will mean that I'll be able to have kids someday. I've always wanted a lot of kids."

Tom nodded and inwardly smiled. This morning, he had never said two words to this girl. And now they were discussing a woman's period.

"You have three sisters?" she asked.

"And no brothers. I think that's why my dad put me in football at a young age. He wanted to make sure my sisters didn't have undue influence over me...or something."

"It must be neat to have three sisters."

"Sure, I guess, but I don't get much time in the bathroom. I've got to either get up two hours early or take my shower at night."

Despite all that had happened, Jenny offered a guarded smile. Her eyes were the most attractive shade of ivy green. "How about you? Any brothers or sisters?"

"I'm adopted. My mom and dad weren't able to have any kids of their own."

"Oh." He hesitated, then said, "Hey, I'm sorry to hear about your dad."

"My mom misses him. It's been hard on her."

"It must be hard on you too."

He saw her eyes well up with tears. She nodded. "Well, I'd better go." She touched the handle of the car door. Tom got out, ran around to her side and opened up the door for her. As she got out, she pointed to the sweater, still tied around her waist. "I'll wash this for you."

"If you want to."

"Yes, I want to. Thanks again."

"Hey, no problem. I'm glad I could help. See you tomorrow?"

Jenny cringed, her shoulders slumping.

"Did I say something wrong?"

"I wonder if the school would notice if I didn't come in for the next week. Perhaps then everyone will forget."

"You know what? How about I come and pick you up and drive you to school? Then we can go in together and anyone who teases you will have to deal with me."

"Thank you. That's very kind of you."

"You know us football types, we can be intimidating when we need to be."

She smiled, then said, "See you tomorrow."

She walked, then turned back and mouthed the words "Thank you." Tom waved, then drove off.

Tom watched enough police shows on television to know that most kidnapping victims are killed within the first 24 hours. A sob crept up Tom's throat and he forced it back down. He needed to focus on the road in front of him.

Eight

Denise Kramer drove in the passing lane on the Queensway about five kilometers from the exit that would bring her to the cabin when she noticed a blue van speeding in the other direction. "That jerk's gonna kill someone," she muttered.

Her thoughts turned to the cottage that would be her home for the next week or so. It seemed ironic that the only thing they used this cabin for was when Lou went hunting with his friends. When they got divorced, Lou agreed to give Denise the cabin, if she gave up any interest in the two trucks and his retirement fund. She had planned to sell it, then reconsidered. Denise was now thankful that she had such an out-of-the-way place to take Jenny. She hung a right at the next exit and drove towards Cedar Lake. Denise found herself relaxing against the seat. *Only five more kilometers to the cottage.*

Denise reached down to change the radio station, then looked up. Steam was coming from under the hood. Glancing down, she saw that the temperature gauge was in the red zone. She swore under her breath and slammed the wheel with her hands. Could she drive the five kilometers or not? She had forgotten what Lou had said about that.

She decided that she had better stop, so she pulled along the side of the road. She should've listened to Lou and not bought a Ford, which, according to her ex-husband, stood for "Fix or repair daily." Nervously, she looked in the back seat at the unconscious woman. Perhaps she could figure out what was wrong with the stupid car before anyone came along.

She yanked on the lever to open the hood. Thankfully, the road was quiet, no cars coming in either direction. After impatiently waiting a few minutes for the engine to cool down, she got out and lifted the hood. Leaning in, she noticed that the overflow tank was bone dry which meant that there was little or no coolant left inside the radiator. It would be too dangerous to open the radiator right now. She knew that she could probably make it to the cottage, but she would have to keep an eye on the temperature gauge. There was probably spare coolant in the storage shed beside the cottage. She shut the hood and walked around the car to the driver's side. Now she would have to wait ten minutes or so before driving.

Hearing the faint rumble of traffic, Denise looked up. That's when she saw the car coming in the opposite direction and slowing down on the other side of the road. Panic set in. Her heart was now racing and her hands trembling. "Get a hold of yourself, Dee," she whispered. "You can handle this." The car hadn't stopped yet.

She quickly opened the door behind the driver's seat, reached down onto the floor for a blanket and hurriedly threw it over the unconscious woman. As she frantically did so, behind her, a car door opened and shut. Footsteps approached. She slammed the door, turned, and placed her body in front of the back window. Raising her head, she smiled at the young man walking towards her. He was casually dressed in a golf shirt with green khaki shorts and his hair was badly in need of a cut.

"You need any help?" he asked.

"Uh...no, I don't think so," Denise answered, trying to make her voice sound even and in control. "The radiator just needs some coolant."

"I've got coolant in my trunk, if you'd like some."

"No, I'll be fine. My place is only five kilometers up the road."

"Okay, take it easy," he said, then smiled and returned to his car. She stayed by the side of the car and watched the man drive away.

After ten minutes had passed, she got behind the wheel, released a long sigh and began to drive.

Soon, Denise was driving up the winding dirt road to the cabin. Frequently checking the temperature gauge, she could see that it was quickly approaching the red section, so she stepped on the accelerator. She was going to make it.

The cabin sat on a slight hill and she had to put her car into third gear in order to make it up the rest of the incline. She pulled the car in front of the cabin and, for a moment, left the unconscious Jenny in the back seat while she went in and finished preparing the room.

She trudged up the porch, unlocked the door, and stepped into the living room. Despite the sweeping and scrubbing she gave it last week, the place smelled moldy and musty. To the left of the small living room was the door to the bedroom. To the right was the small kitchenette. In the middle of the living room was an old wood stove. A La-Z-Boy chair faced a television at the far wall. The home birth and baby materials were stacked against the wall near the bedroom door.

She opened up the windows in the living room, then turned her attention to the bedroom. The chains were already bolted to the metal cot and the pail placed on the floor nearby.

Denise returned to the car and swung open the back door. She reached in and slid Jenny out partway. She took a deep breath, then lifted her up and out of the car. She was heavy, and Denise now understood the term "dead weight."

She half-carried, half-dragged her. Denise's feet sunk into the moist ground with the extra weight of Jenny's pregnant body. When she reached the porch, she grunted with each step as she lifted the girl. She carefully placed her right foot on the top step and gasped as her foot dropped through part of the rotting wood, slamming her against the outside log wall. She remained still for a moment, wondering whether the girl in her arms would rouse. Despite the jarring movement, Jenny was out cold.

Denise's left foot thankfully had remained on the step

below. She yanked her foot from the hole and lifted it up higher to step onto the porch, using the wall to gain her balance.

She shuffled along the porch, stepping carefully in case there were any other rotting pieces of wood, and finally reached the door. Inside, she dragged Jenny to the bedroom and practically dropped her onto the cot. Jenny let out a breath and a quiet moan, but remained unconscious.

Kneeling beside the cot, Denise pulled Jenny over onto her right side and clasped the cuff around Jenny's left ankle. As she did so, she noticed the woman's swollen feet. She tugged on the chain to make sure it was secure, then stretched it out to make sure it could reach the pail several feet away.

Denise picked up the woman's two hands and handcuffed them together to the metal post of the cot. Denise slid the pail closer to the bed, then slowly peeled the tape from the girl's mouth.

Memory loss and hallucinations were also known to be side effects of Ketamine. Denise had no idea how Jenny was going to react to being in a strange place and having been kidnapped by a strange woman...and hallucinations and amnesia on top of that? No telling how hysterical she might be...which is why she brought the Diazepam.

Denise returned to the car and retrieved the extra provisions: some magazines, today's newspaper and a few candy bars. She was also desperately in need of a cigarette, so she lit one up and breathed in, her eyes closing and her heart slowing.

It occurred to her that she could probably use a good stiff drink. She reconsidered. She needed to be sober right now.

"Here, have one more drink," the boy said. He was awfully nice, although Denise couldn't remember his name. She swallowed the whole glass, the fluid burning her throat.

The boy kissed her, then started to unbutton her blouse. Her mind was rather cloudy, and she was finding it hard to think straight. But Denise knew that she liked him — he was cute — and, most importantly, she wanted him to like her.

Denise switched on the TV and channel surfed. It had been less than an hour since she kidnapped Jenny and there was no news yet about the kidnapping. She scowled and continued to search.

Nine

As Tom turned onto his street, he could barely maneuver his van through the already narrow road. News vans, several police cars, and a large crowd of neighbors had already gathered in front of his house. *This is a nightmare, a horrible nightmare, and I'm going to wake up and both Jen and I will laugh about it.*

The van screeched as he turned into his driveway and he nearly slammed into his mother's car. He got out and the flashes of several cameras struck him like small hands across his face. A reporter shoved an iPod in front of his mouth. "Are you the missing woman's husband?"

"Yes, yes, I am. I need to be with my children. Get out of my way."

Faceless people surrounded him in a claustrophobic wall. More flashes exploded in his face, cameras, cell phones pointed at him. He pushed his way through the crowd to the front door. From behind him, he heard, "Mr. Callahan, are you a suspect in your wife's disappearance?"

Tom stopped and slammed his foot down, then turned toward the voice. "No, I am not a suspect in my wife's disappearance, you...I love my wife and this..." As he was speaking, someone had grabbed a hold of his suit jacket and was tugging him toward the house. Tom looked around and saw that it was a tall, nicely dressed woman. "Give Mr. Callahan some privacy, please."

He finally made it inside the front door and the door slammed behind him. He could hear Bootsie barking from somewhere inside the house.

"Where are my kids? I need to see my children." He began to hyperventilate, then he tried to breathe slowly.

"Tom." His mother joined him in the overcrowded foyer. She put her hand on his shoulder. "The children are eating their dinner in the kitchen. They're fine."

"Mr. Callahan?"

The tall, well-dressed woman spoke in a calm voice, "My name is Sergeant Kathy Romano of the OPP and I'm in charge of the investigation into the disappearance of your wife. I know this is a difficult time, but if I could just ask you a couple of questions..."

"Can't it wait? I want to see..."

"Mr. Callahan, the more information we gather, the more likely we can find your wife quickly."

"Yes, all right," he said, dropping down onto the bottom step of the staircase.

"Mr. Callahan, do you know anyone that might want to harm your wife?"

"Absolutely not. Jenny doesn't have any enemies. I mean, people think we're crazy because we have a lot of kids, but, no enemies."

"Can you tell us where you were today at 3:00 p.m?"

"At my office. Oh, man. Do you think I could've..."

"No, Mr. Callahan, but the sooner we eliminate you as a suspect..."

"A suspect...how can I possibly...."

"In a case like this, everyone's a suspect. We just need to rule you out."

"There are 30 people who work in that office. They can all vouch for my presence."

"Thank you. What is it that you do, sir?"

"I'm an accountant at McNeil and Smythe on Kent Street in Ottawa. Look, my wife is missing and...she's pregnant. She's due in a week, so you need to find her!"

"Do you remember what your wife was wearing this morning?"

Tom tried to recall. Was she still wearing her robe? No, he was sure she was dressed, but couldn't remember what she was wearing. "Sorry, I can't."

"Okay."

"But she usually wears maternity jeans."

"Jeans, good. Thank you, Mr. Callahan."

"Oh, and Jen has a cell phone. Is there any way you can find it? She never goes anywhere without it. I've been calling her since I left work."

"I know this is still early in the investigation, Mr. Callahan..."

"Call me Tom, please."

"Tom, was your wife depressed?"

"On the contrary. She was excited about the baby. She's had three miscarriages. I mean, I know we already have five kids, but Jen was heartbroken and really, really wanted this baby."

"I see."

"She didn't just leave. She would never, ever do something like that, tie our son to a pole and leave."

"I needed to ask the question, just to rule it out."

He nodded.

"The OPP will be organizing a press conference. Would you be interested in making a statement? Whoever abducted your wife might be watching the news."

Tom shook his head. A press conference? His wife kidnapped? Surely this had to be a nightmare from which he would wake up soon.

"Does your wife own a computer or laptop?"

"We have a family laptop in the kitchen."

"Would I have your permission to take it?"

"Yes, sure, sure. Take whatever you need to find her."

"Is there a password on here?"

Tom wrote down the password on a piece of paper and handed it to Sergeant Romano.

"And I'd like to take a look at your bedroom and search through her drawers, if I have your permission to do that?"

"Yes, yes, fine." He got off the step and stood beside the sergeant. He pointed up the stairs. "Our bedroom is the one on the right at the top."

"Thanks.   The OPP will be stationing a constable to remain here around the clock in case there is a ransom call."

"Ransom?"

"Yes. There may be a ransom. Constable Anderson will be staying until his shift ends at midnight.   There will be another officer assigned to stay until he returns in the morning. The calls will be monitored and recorded from the OPP Detachment."

Out of the corner of his eye, Tom saw a man approaching them.

The officer held out his hand.   Tom shook it and glanced at the man's face.   He looked vaguely familiar. "Constable Anderson?"

"Yes. Tom, I don't know if you remember me, but...."

Suddenly, Tom recognized the annoying jerk that made fun of his wife in high school. He stepped back and frowned. "You're a police officer now?"

"Yes. I'm sorry that we had to see each other under such difficult circumstances. I want you to know I'm praying for the safe return of your wife."

Tom shrugged. "I need to see my kids."

He rushed past his mother and the two officers and into the kitchen. "Daddy, Daddy, home," Caleb squealed.

"Yes, Sport, Dad's home."   He picked up his son.

"Mommy gone."

"Yes, but we're going to find her."

"Daddy," Chris held onto her father and began to sob.

"Hey, hey, honey, we're going to find her."

Callie and Cassie latched on tightly to his legs. Chloe held her arms up. Tom's eyes caught sight of their photo from high school on the wall in front of him. "Cutest couple, SHS class of '99."

The photographer motioned for Tom to sit on a chair, then asked Jenny to sit on Tom's lap. At the request, Jenny looked at Tom, then lowered her head. "Perhaps she can sit beside me?" Tom asked the photographer, who indicated yes.

"Hey, Red, act as if you like her," the photographer cajoled. Tom put his arm around her, protectively, and she cocked her head and smiled.

Tom sighed, his heart heavy. *Please God, keep Jen and the baby safe.*

* * *

Kathy climbed the stairs and perused the family photos along the wall, some candid shots, others posed. One particular photo near the top of the steps drew her attention and she stopped to study it more closely. It was of a young, beautiful, teenage Jenny, sitting on a rock in a park somewhere, the rich autumn yellow, orange and red colors in the background. Jenny's long brown hair reminded Kathy of photos of herself as a preteen in the 70's. Her bright eyes and wide smile made Kathy want to keep staring at it.

Kathy made her way toward the largest bedroom. The upstairs of the Callahan house had slanted ceilings, so Kathy found herself crouching so she wouldn't hit the low ceiling. She reached inside her coat jacket and tugged on a pair of disposable latex gloves. It was a small room made even smaller by the queen-sized bed in the middle. The blue and yellow-flowered quilt was hastily laid across it. A dresser with a mirror lined the left wall, a small end table edged the bed and another taller dresser lined the right wall, beside the window.

The dresser with the mirror was cluttered, to say the least. A few religious pictures had been tucked into the bottom edge of the mirror, a jewelry box in the center and two photos of the family flanked it. The photos and jewelry box were difficult to see with the pile of clothes, what looked like women's underwear, socks and tee shirts stacked at various spots on the dresser.

She began to open drawers. Normally, when the victim was confirmed dead, Kathy didn't feel as if she were intruding. But here, with Jenny Callahan hopefully still alive, she felt like she was peering into the young woman's most intimate thoughts and possessions. Kathy dismissed the thought and tried to focus on the task at hand.

More underwear and socks in the top drawer, shirts and pajamas in the second drawer and pants in the bottom. Clothes were folded but not neatly; exactly what she'd expect of a pregnant woman with five kids. She moved garments around, not knowing what she was searching for.

Next, she scanned the rest of the room. The top of the night stand nearest that dresser was a hodge podge of various items, a novel, splayed open, upside down, rosary beads, a brush. A crucifix hung on the wall above the bed. She opened up the top drawer to find a digital thermometer, and a chart with a temperature graph. From looking at the rosaries, crucifix and charts, Kathy surmised that Tom and Jenny were devout Catholics.

Kathy stared at the items. "Who has taken you, Jenny? And where are you?"

Ten

Jenny soared through the clouds like an eagle. The air blew against her face and it smelled like rain and springtime. Strange thing, though. She was lying on her side on a bed or cot of some type. As she floated, the cot slowed down and she saw a bearded man hovering above her. She stared at his handsome face and his cerulean blue eyes.

"Be not afraid, Jenny." The man's voice was deep and calm with kindness radiating from his eyes. For the moment, she wasn't afraid. After all, this was a dream, wasn't it? But this man was so beautiful and so radiant that it was difficult to actually look at him without squinting. Then a realization. Was she dead? She reached her hand out to try to touch him and realized that she couldn't move her arms. She pulled and yanked but could not budge them. Perhaps if she woke herself up, she might be able to move her hands. Then another realization hit her. Her eyes were open and beyond the clouds sat a small table and a pail. She drew in a breath.

You're not going crazy, you're not going crazy. There must be a reasonable explanation for this. Her heart was now pounding a mile a minute. She breathed in deeply through her nose, closed her eyes, then opened them. Same small table, same metal pail, but now instead of clouds, there was a worn hardwood floor.

She strained to keep her eyes open and tried to think of the last thing she remembered. She recalled reading to Caleb on the couch, but couldn't seem to remember anything else. The bus stop. She was supposed to meet the girls at the bus stop. Did she ever make it there? And where were her children?

She dozed off, then woke with a gasp. Jenny tried to sit up and realized that her hands were cuffed to the underside of the cot, so she remained on her side and kept still for the moment. She looked around the room, twisting her head to see the area behind and her eyes widened. She pulled on her ankle and felt the chain. *Oh, dear God in heaven, where am I?*

Jenny had no idea what time it was, although it wasn't yet dark. Judging by the light in the room, she guessed it had to be around 6:00 p.m.

Every bone, every muscle in her body ached. She immediately thought of her unborn child. *How are you doing in there, Little Buddy?* He seemed still, too still for this time of day. *God, please let my baby be okay.*

Her head throbbed. The place smelled like cigarettes and it felt as if her bladder would burst. Her mouth felt tingly. Deep within her stomach, she knew that she was going to vomit.

Jenny tried desperately to concentrate on not throwing up. She had successfully distracted herself in the past several months when the feeling of nausea came upon her. She had no choice but to do that now. However, the more that she tried not to vomit, the stronger the nausea welled up within her. Immediately she threw up the last bit of her grilled cheese lunch all down the front of her and all over the cot, the odor pungent.

The door swung open and Jenny could hear the heavy footsteps of someone approaching her. Jenny kept still, her body facing away from the person. Her heart was racing and her hands were trembling inside the cuffs. *God, please help me.*

When the person came into view, Jenny began to shake. The woman was scowling and she swore under her breath, then stomped out of the room. She looked vaguely familiar, but Jenny couldn't remember where she had seen her.

Seconds later, she returned with a wet cloth. She made a meager attempt at wiping the bed, then roughly wiped Jenny's face and shirt off, all the while keeping silent. The cloth smelled sour, like it had dried but not been rinsed.

The woman kicked the pail closer to the bed.

"Please take me home. My family must be sick with worry."

The woman shrugged, but said nothing.

"I have to... use the bathroom."

Her captor marched over to the headboard, her footsteps loud and heavy. Lifting out a key from her pocket, she unlocked the handcuffs around Jenny's wrists. She turned and left, slamming the door behind her.

Jenny rubbed her wrists and sat up. The room was spinning. She closed her eyes for a moment to allow herself time to adjust. She slowly stood up and walked over to the pail. Part of her wanted to cry, not so much at having to relieve herself in such a way, but at the whole horrible situation. Tom and the kids must be worried and upset. She wanted so much to be able to tell him, *I'm okay, Tom. Don't worry. I'm going to get out of this. I'm going to be fine.* But she wasn't convinced.

After finishing her task, she returned to the cot. At least she didn't have the cuffs on her hands now. The television news was blaring in another room, but she couldn't hear what, if any, information the newscaster gave. Whatever it was, she was sure that the police, Tom, anybody, had to be on their way to rescue her from this madwoman.

Eleven

The local OPP Detachment office in Sutherland was too small to accommodate the extra officers and others who had come forward to help, so an incident command post was set up at the church hall next door.

Kathy placed Tom and Jenny's laptop on the makeshift desk and turned it on just as one constable knocked into her. She took a sip of coffee. Bob Preston dropped a tray of sandwiches in the middle of the desk. "Thanks," she replied. "I haven't been thinking much about eating."

She quickly checked the history and the most recent emails before handing it over to the IT officer to perform a more detailed investigation.

It was already a circus in the building, with reporters, police officers and dozens of people inquiring whether there was any way they could assist. It was one of the things Kathy enjoyed most about working in a small town: everyone working together. Kathy suggested that several officers begin to organize groups of people to search the area. She suspected that whoever took Jenny would not have stayed in town, but it was important to follow every lead. In a situation like this people wanted to help, and this seemed like the ideal way to keep people occupied.

Kathy had ordered another officer to redial Jenny's phone until they could triangulate the signal and locate it. In the interim, a passerby had picked the phone up. The passerby was asked to wait there, as the phone was evidence in an investigation.

She and Bob Preston immediately proceeded to where crime scene tape had already been placed around the area of the cell phone. As she stood beside Bob, she stifled an urge to ask him if he was standing in a hole. Bob wasn't sensitive about his short stature and, in any other situation, Kathy would have joked with him about it.

However, this was no time for joviality.

Unfortunately, the cyclist who had discovered the cell phone had not only picked up the phone, but had continued to hold onto it until the police arrived. So much for undisturbed evidence. The cell phone had already been bagged and was on its way to the OPP crime lab.

Crime scene investigators were already photographing the car tracks. She crossed the street and crouched down to study the area where the cell phone had been discovered.

Bob Preston approached her. "The man from the Forensic Identification Unit says there are also some shoe prints, perhaps size 8, running shoe of some kind. They're photographing, then making plaster molds of those tracks as well."

"Good. Make sure the FIU checks for fingerprints and tell them I need the report ASAP."

* * *

Despite the constant nausea, Jenny's stomach began to growl. She hadn't yet been offered anything to eat, but God knows what that woman would give her anyway. What if there was something in the food to harm to her? Despite the hunger pangs, her stomach was turned inside out with fear. What was this woman going to do with her? Little Buddy took a stretch within her, but still seemed quieter than usual. She stared at her large belly. *What if she wants Little Buddy?*

In the last two hours, bits and pieces of memory had started to return. Jenny now remembered walking to the bus stop and meeting the woman there.

Then a realization. That woman was pregnant. So why was she doing this? And where had she seen her before?

The blinds were drawn, the window closed, although a sliver of light streamed in through the bottom. Jenny was starting to feel warm. It wasn't an unusually hot day, but it became difficult to breathe. The air in the room smelled musty, like it hadn't been circulated for many years.

Jenny surmised the kidnapper was a chain smoker. Even though the door was shut, the air was thick with cigarette smoke, which worsened Jenny's nausea. She hated the smell, although when she was younger and growing up with two parents who smoked, she had been used to it. Thankfully, after her dad died of lung cancer, her mom promptly quit.

The door swung open and Jenny turned to face her captor, who dropped a TV dinner on the small table beside the cot. Jenny stared at the woman's middle.

"Please let me go. Why are you doing this?"

She hurried out of the room and slammed the door without speaking.

Jenny pleaded, her voice now high pitched. "My family must be sick with worry. Please, let me call my husband and let him know I'm all right. Please!"

Jenny lowered her head. She missed Tom so much. Although he wasn't perfect and had made his own share of mistakes over the years, Tom had been her knight in shining armor on more than a few occasions.

Thirteen years earlier

Jenny snuggled up close to Tom as they sat in the front seat of the car. She knew that she would have to go inside in a few minutes, but relished these quiet moments with him. Her head was against Tom's chest and his arm was around her shoulder. She could smell the smoky scent of the bonfire on his jacket. They had just come back from a party at his friend's cottage, where the group had toasted marshmallows and sung campfire songs. His friend, Kevin, had invited everyone to come inside. "There are enough rooms for every couple here," Kevin announced, winking. Tom had glanced at Jenny awkwardly and whispered, "I had no idea, Jen." She had nodded, then watched the other couples move into the house. Tom had stood and cleared his throat. "We're going to head out," he told Kevin. "Come on," *Kevin had pleaded with him. Tom had smiled, politely declined, then accompanied Jen to the car.*

They said little on the way to her house. When he stopped the car, Tom pulled Jen close. "I love you, Jen."

"I love you too, Tom."

"Well...I have a confession to make."

Jenny lifted her head and stared at him. Although it was dark, the street lamp lit up the car and she could see his face clearly. He could not look her in the eye.

"I...well, I..."

"What?"

"I lied. I had heard through the grapevine that Kevin might pull that stunt. I suppose a part of me wanted to have you alone, even for a few hours."

She opened her mouth to say something, then reconsidered. She and Tom had spent most of their days together, not only in school, but after football practice and on weekends. Her status and popularity skyrocketed now that she was a football player's girlfriend. Not that she cared, of course, but life had become different from the first few lonely days of school here in Ontario.

"Are you angry with me, Jen?"

She shook her head. She wasn't angry, just disappointed. They had only been dating for a few months, but trust had been an integral part of their relationship. They had even begun attending Mass together. She had assumed that Tom was on the same page as she was, but perhaps she was wrong.

Tom kissed the top of her head, then the side of her face. They began to kiss then Jenny pulled away.

"I love you, Tom, but I won't...do that. I made a promise last year at a chastity rally that I would wait until marriage."

He exhaled, but said nothing.

"I suppose you didn't make that same promise, eh?"

"Well..."

"*How about making that promise to me then?*"

"*Yes, all right.*" He said it quickly, without hesitation and, for a split second, Jenny wondered if he just said it to please her.

"*Really?*"

"*Yes, really.*" He leaned down. She was kissing him and again felt safe in his arms.

The TV dinner sat on the table, condensation forming under the plastic covering the sections. Jenny groaned. She didn't care for TV dinners, but wasn't about to complain.

Jenny now had an even more pressing concern than her hunger. Jenny's stomach clenched as she recalled staring at her captor's mid-section just moments earlier. That woman was most definitely *not* pregnant.

* * *

Tom was still wearing his dress clothes from work, but he had taken off his tie and noosed it around the back of his chair at the kitchen table. His mother had fed the kids earlier so he sat alone.

She dished out some sort of casserole, but he was in no mood for eating. It smelled and looked like some sort of turkey concoction which, on a normal day, would probably have been very tasty. But this wasn't a normal day, and as he leaned over the plate, his stomach felt queasy. The phone rang and Jeff gave the thumbs up sign before Tom clicked "talk" on his cordless phone. It was strange having him listen in to every conversation. "Hello?"

"Tom? This is Sam."

"Hey, Sam." It was good to hear his friend's voice.

"I just heard about Jenny. I tried calling your cell phone but you weren't picking up. I also emailed you but figured with all that was going on, you might not be checking email. I hope it's okay to call you."

"Of course. I think I left my cell phone in the van. I wasn't thinking clearly when I pulled up...there were so many news vans and reporters, I couldn't see the house. And you're right, I'm not checking email."

"Is there anything I can do? Do you want me to come over?"

Tom took a deep breath then let it out. "I don't think so, but I do appreciate the call. I just can't believe this."

"Me neither. Hang in there. They'll find her."

"Thanks."

* * *

Denise set up the army cot beside the chair. She probably should have bought a more comfortable (and more expensive) cot, but this would have to suffice for the time being. After all, she wouldn't be here that long.

The cute boy with the dreamy eyes coaxed Denise down into the basement. His parents were gone for the night, or so he said. Their first time together was on an old army cot that had cobwebs on it and smelled funny. She let him do whatever he wanted because he treated her special. Of course, afterwards, he told her that she would have to leave. The next day at school, he acted like he didn't know her. After school, he caught up with her as she walked home and invited her back. She didn't like that he acted as if he didn't know her. But he was cute, so she agreed to go back to his house.

Denise imagined that she wouldn't be getting much sleep tonight anyway, not with the excitement and her desire to watch the news constantly. She sat up and turned up the volume on the television. Depending on the station, some of the newscasters were issuing updates on the kidnapping every 15 minutes.

She laid the blanket on top of the cot, then returned to the chair and sat down. Denise was pleasantly surprised that Jenny wasn't more hysterical. She was upset — that was obvious — but who wouldn't be in her situation?

The fake pregnant belly that she had been wearing for the past few months now took up space on the small kitchen counter. She was glad to have the stupid thing off as it was becoming uncomfortable. And no one was going to see her out here anyway, so it wasn't necessary to continue the charade.

She lit up a cigarette, sat back and continued to watch the news.

* * *

Tom piled all five kids into his and Jen's queen-sized bed and one by one, they fell asleep. Chris was the last to drop off. *Always a worrier, that one.* She seemed "old" when she was three, speaking in full sentences, reading by the time she was four. Chris was the natural born leader of the Callahan kids, and almost never had to be asked to do a job or to help out with her younger siblings.

Little Caleb snorted and turned over on Tom's chest.

Tom realized that none of them would get any sleep unless they were together. His mom had offered to stay the night and help put the kids to bed. He told her that she could stay, but he declined her offer to put the children to sleep as he wanted to do that.

His mother slept in Chris and Chloe's room. Earlier this evening, she had scowled, then snorted when she saw the mess of the room. He couldn't help it. With all the stress and worry about Jen, he finally yelled at his mom. And not just yelled. He went on for two minutes telling her that if she didn't like the mess, she could leave. He was grateful that she didn't leave. A few minutes later, he apologized, but his mom remained quiet for the remainder of the evening.

His stomach was in knots every time he thought about the way he spoke to his wife earlier that morning. If something happens to her and the baby, he would not be able to forgive himself. And it was probably the reason he lashed out at his mom, since she was often a sore point in their marriage.

When he found out that there were groups that had started to search the area for his wife, Tom called Sergeant Romano. He wanted to join in the search or help at the OPP Detachment, anything, to keep himself busy. At least then he would feel like something was being accomplished. But she had told him to stay put, take care of the kids, and leave the searching and investigating to the police.

The small reading lamp at the bedside table on Jen's side of the bed was on. The novel she was reading lay open and facing down. The cordless phone lay still and unmoving beside it. Jen's hairbrush and rosary were next to the phone. How could something so horrible be happening to them right now?

Jeff Anderson, officially now Constable Anderson, left at eleven. Another officer — Tom forgot his name — took his place a short while ago.

It was ironic that, of all people, Jeff would be the police officer assigned to stay with his family. He was a jerk in high school who caused Jenny so much grief.

Earlier today, however, Jeff appeared genuinely contrite, going so far as to say that he was praying for her safe return. Evidently, he had changed.

Tom lay awake staring at the ceiling. Years of football taught him to ignore physical aches, but how was he supposed to ignore the emotional turmoil his heart and soul were enduring?

He reached over, trying not to wake Caleb on his chest, and switched the small lamp off. The bed, his old bed from home, squeaked as he moved. It didn't bother him, but Jen was forever nagging him to oil whatever was squeaking.

Their bedroom was the largest room on the second floor. The queen-sized bed, one small night table and two chests of drawers were squeezed into the room. But Jen never complained. In fact, she frequently told Tom that she loved this house and, despite the size, could see herself growing old in it. He, on the other hand, pictured their six children in ten year's time and thought they should move to a larger home when the mortgage was paid off in seven years.

He wondered what would happen to the growing crowd on the narrow street in front of their house. It was only a matter of time before neighbors started to complain. *To hell with them. To hell with the neighbors and Jeff Anderson and the news programs.* Then, from deep inside him, he realized that he could not harbor that attitude. He couldn't get angry with the neighbors or the newscasters or the police officers. They didn't abduct his wife.

Chloe snuggled up closer to Tom's arm; the older girls were packed like sardines on either sides of him. Thankfully, the news vans seemed quiet, although at last glance, there were more than ten now parked on the street.

His mother-in-law had called earlier and informed him that she was taking the first plane out from Saskatchewan. Of all the times for Jen's mother to be out of town, this seemed to be the worst. He knew that Susan didn't really want to leave Jen so close to her delivery, and she had agonized over whether she ought to go. In the end, both Tom and Jen had encouraged her to make the trip and take care of her sister.

He stretched his legs and heard a grunt from Bootsie, who had taken up her usual position at the foot of the bed.

Not knowing was the worst part for him. He had no idea where the kidnapper had taken her, if she was hungry, in pain. And yet, the not knowing, the uncertainty, still held hope and he clung to it.

"I should pray," he said, and he carefully reached over and lifted off Jen's rosary from the bedside table. *...He was crucified, died and was buried.* He blinked his eyes. He tried hard to control his emotions; he didn't want to wake the kids who had finally fallen asleep and were all breathing deeply. *God, I just can't pray right now. Please, please keep Jen and Little Buddy safe...*

Twelve

On the evening edition of the local news, the newscaster reported that they were looking for a woman in connection with the "abduction." Denise wasn't worried. In fact, she liked the idea that she was famous. Of course, once Jenny gave birth, she'd take the baby and disappear into oblivion. If Jenny didn't give birth within the next few days, Denise would just have to use Pitocin to induce labor. She took comfort knowing that she had enough Sleepaway to put Jenny out for good afterwards.

Denise didn't want to see Jenny suffer needlessly. She knew from personal experience that being on the receiving end of someone's fist was not a way to get someone to cooperate. If Denise had really wanted Jenny to suffer, she would've just taken the baby already. Instead, she had made sure that Jenny was in a cot, had a pail to relieve herself, and was given food when needed.

Jenny was quiet for now. Denise had given her a TV dinner. She had made two of them, one for her and one for Jenny. It wasn't half bad either: turkey, mashed potatoes and a mouthful of cake for dessert.

She lit a cigarette and watched the last 20 minutes of *Law & Order*. She laughed under her breath. Her kidnapping of Jenny could actually be one of those episodes.

Denise jumped at the sound of her cell phone ringing. She wasn't even sure there would be reception out here. And no one rang her cell phone, except for twice a year when her cousin, Anne, didn't know where she was.

"Hello."

"Hey, Dee, where are you? I tried the house and --"

"I had an emergency...a friend needed some help and I'm staying with her."

"Did you hear the news? A pregnant woman went missing near you."

"Really?"

"Yeah, haven't you heard about it?"

"I think I heard something about it on the TV. Anne, would you do me a favor and check on Fritz? I left enough food to last a week, but could you check on him every day until I return, perhaps let him out in the yard?"

Her cousin hesitated. "Yeah, sure, Dee. How long will you be gone?"

"Not too sure." Denise could see that the local news was just coming on. She covered the phone, "Yeah, all right, I'm coming," she said, then took her hand off the phone. "Gotta go. Call you in a few days, okay?"

She flipped the phone closed, and leaned forward to turn up the volume on the television.

"A Sutherland woman was abducted today from a school bus stop. Jennifer Callahan, seen in this photo, is 29 and is nine months pregnant with her sixth child. If you have seen this woman or you have information regarding her disappearance or whereabouts, please call the following number."

Denise looked at the photo. She marveled at how happy they all seemed. The picture had to be over a year old because Jenny, with her long brown hair pulled back off her face, was not noticeably pregnant. The four girls were dressed in identical green-patterned dresses. The boy was in a similarly colored jumper and looked to be about two.

"Well, isn't that sweet, even the boy had something that matches the girls....and everybody's so damned happy. I bet they're not so happy now."

Why couldn't I have had a happy family? Everyone had had a happy childhood except for Denise. Her aunt and uncle merely tolerated her presence. In some ways, the foster home held happier memories. Children's Aid thought "relatives" would be better for her. That first night at her aunt and uncle's place, she woke up crying because she had wet the bed. Instead of being consoled, she was forced to sleep on a cheap mattress on the floor for the next few years.

* * *

Jenny woke to the sound of a cell phone ringing. This time, it was dark — pitch black — to be more precise. The only light was a line under the bedroom door. She could still hear the TV in the background, although Jenny couldn't tell which channel or show it was.

She again felt sick to her stomach, but thankfully, at least her wrist was no longer chained to the bed. This could be worse. "Yeah, how?" Jenny asked herself out loud. "My legs are chained to a bolt in the floor, I've been laying in my own vomit for several hours now, I have a headache, I have to pee in a bucket..."

Answering herself, she admitted, "I'm alive. I must remember that. I'm alive and my baby..." Suddenly, Jenny realized that she wasn't sure the last time the baby had moved.

For a moment, she panicked, pressing her stomach roughly. "Come on, Little Buddy, let me know you're all right." No response. She poked him again, trying to push the baby inside of her. Her heart started beating rapidly, her breath became shallow. *No, God, please, not that.* Finally, Little Buddy reacted to her nudge and stretched. *Thank you, God.*

She made the sign of the cross and began the prayers of the rosary.

* * *

Kathy checked the call history on Jenny Callahan's cell phone. The last outgoing call was to Tom Callahan's work number, two days ago. The last 45 incoming calls were from Tom's cell phone, all calls unanswered and each one about 20 to 30 seconds apart. Three partial prints were found on it, and were currently being analyzed by the RCMP.

Thirteen

September 10th

"Daddy, wake up?"

Tom opened his eyes. Caleb's round face was practically on top of his. He grunted. Guilt rose in him and stung his throat. How could he have fallen asleep when Jen was out there, missing, perhaps hurt? Tom didn't know how long he had slept, but it couldn't have been more than an hour. Still, he shouldn't have slept at all.

He squinted at the clock radio and saw that it was six a.m. The sun was just coming up, the birds already singing. *How can they sing like that when Jen's missing?*

"Hungy, Dad. 'ave Kispies?" Caleb's nose was touching Tom's. His son no longer had the sweet milk breath of a baby and toddler, but ordinary kid morning breath. When had that happened?

"All right, Caleb."

Their chatter caused the girls to rouse. "It's early," complained Cassie.

"You guys go back to sleep. I'm going to get your brother some cereal."

Chris was already up and putting on her robe. She followed her dad and picked up Caleb.

He glanced down the hallway and out the window at the street below. No surprise. More news vans. He couldn't tell, but it appeared as if they now took up both sides of the street. He cringed. He followed Chris and Caleb down the stairs.

Once in the kitchen, he smiled to the police officer, a middle-aged man, who was reading a newspaper.

As Chris got Caleb a bowl of cereal, Tom busied himself with the task of making coffee. Momentarily, the daily routine kept him distracted. His daughter poured milk into the bowl for her brother. All of a sudden, the enormity of the whole situation caused his shoulders to slump. How could this be happening? How was he supposed to just keep going?

"Mommy comin' home, Dad?" Caleb's small voice questioned. Tom forced a smile. "Yeah, Sport, they're gonna find Mommy and she'll be home soon."

He glanced at Chris. She was looking at him with her big brown eyes, the ones which prompted him to say yes every time she asked for something. He couldn't say yes this time.

Tom wondered what time he should wake the other girls up, then decided that he would let them sleep in. He had spoken to his boss last night and the man was very sympathetic.

Part of him wanted to switch on the little TV set in the kitchen. Another part of him couldn't deal with watching news about his family, about Jen. Someone had already given the family photo to the local TV station. At first, he was annoyed. But he softened when he realized that it might help someone to come forward so that Jen might be found.

Another reporter had evidently hacked into Jen's Facebook page and downloaded a few photos of her. His wife assured him that only her "friends" could see her information and view her photos. *So much for private information.*

The house seemed too quiet. Heck, he hated it when Jen took all the kids somewhere because he couldn't stand the "noise" of the silence.

The shrill sound of the phone jolted him. Tom looked at the police officer, who gave him the thumbs up sign to answer the phone. He reached for it and picked it up before it rang a third time.

"Hello?"

"Tom, this is Father Paul. I hope I didn't wake you."

"No, you didn't."

"I just found out about Jenny. I was on retreat and

didn't arrive home until one a.m. I didn't check my messages until now. Many people phoned to tell me that Jenny was missing." He paused. "I'll be saying morning Mass, then I'm coming over. It'll be around 9:00. I just watched a repeat of the news last night and it looks like a circus at your place."

"Yeah, it is, Father. Thanks."

An hour later, shift change took place and Jeff Anderson returned. He offered Tom an awkward smile, then took up his place in the kitchen corner next to the table.

* * *

"Father Paul is here!" the younger girls, now awake, shouted in unison.

They surrounded the young priest, who was holding a travel coffee mug. The children began jumping on him and hugging him.

"Whoa, kids. Hot coffee in my hands. Hang on a minute." He set the coffee down on the small table by the front door, then crouched down to receive hugs from the kids.

Father Paul O'Neill was a few years older than Tom and Jenny and when he wasn't dressed in his priestly outfit, his muscular body made one think that he played football or some other sport for a living.

Father Paul was also child friendly, unlike their previous pastor, an elderly, stiff, 'old school' type who didn't appreciate the baby babbling and toddler talking at Mass.

"Mommy gone."

"Yes, Caleb, I know, but we're praying real hard that your mom is found soon. I'm going to stay with you guys for a while. Is that okay?"

"Yep."

"Chris, take the kids into the living room and turn on a DVD, would you?" Tom asked. She nodded and took her brother's hand.

"Thanks, Father. I appreciate you coming."

"How're you holding up, Tom?"

"As good as can be expected." He paused. "I'm really scared. Jenny's out there with God knows who and..." Tom exhaled.

"What?"

"She's scheduled for a C-section next week because of her condition."

"Right. Isn't that why Jenny has been on bed rest?"

"Yeah. What if she isn't found before the baby comes?"

"Tom, you need to focus on getting her back, not on what can happen if she doesn't come back. There are many, many people praying for her right now."

Tom nodded.

"How did you make it through the swarms of reporters?"

"I pretended I was going for a touchdown, the way I did in college."

Tom allowed himself to smile.

"Daddy, Daddy, come, look at the TV!" Callie called.

Tom rushed into the living room and on the television was one of the early morning shows with a story about Jen's disappearance. He immediately took the controller and changed it to a channel with cartoons.

"There, you guys can watch that."

He walked over to the window, parted the now-drawn drapes and peered outside. CTV, CBC, CNN, Global, NBC, ABC, CBS, Fox News.

"It might be a good idea to give a statement. You never know if Jen will be able to hear it." Father Paul suggested.

"I will be talking to the reporters when Sergeant Romano arrives."

"That's good. When will Jen's mom be arriving?"

Tom checked his watch. "Susan left this morning from Regina. Her plane should be arriving around ten or so. My dad's picking her up from the airport."

Tom's mother, Doris, approached the pair. "Good morning, Father. Can I get you anything?"

"No, I'm fine."

The phone rang. Tom looked toward Constable Anderson, who gave him the thumbs up sign to answer it. He walked away, pressed the talk button and said, "Hello?"

He covered the receiver. "It's Sergeant Romano."

"Yes, all right, around 10:00 would be fine, Sergeant. It'll be a short statement. Yes, thanks." He turned toward the priest. "Sorry about that."

"Don't worry, Tom. I was just heading into the back yard to have a smoke."

"Okay." Tom paused. "You gotta quit smoking."

"Yeah, yeah, I know."

"You're such a great priest; we'd love to see you around for another 50 years."

"Me too, Tom, me too." Father Paul opened the sliding doors and stepped onto the deck. Bootsie decided to take the opportunity to venture outside to do her business.

Doris tapped him on the shoulder. He turned toward her.

"Tom, go take a shower and shave."

"All right, Mom."

As he lathered the shaving cream on his face, Tom's eyes caught sight of the shower stall in the mirror.

"Hey, you almost don't fit in here, big woman."

"You keep talking like that and I'm getting out."

"I'm just kidding. Come on," he said as they embraced. As he kissed her, his stomach against his wife's, the baby kicked him.

"Whoa, Little Buddy is strong."

"Tell me about it."

He recalled Jen's awkwardness and discomfort with

how much weight she had gained after her pregnancy with Caleb. For some reason, she had gained more and hadn't been able to lose the extra weight. He tried to convince her that it didn't matter to him, that he loved her, that he was still attracted to her.

Tom hurriedly rushed through his shaving and, as a result, nicked himself three times. He thought about what he should say when he made a statement to the press.

He stared into the bathroom mirror and started to rehearse. "Please, whoever has Jen, let her go. She's a wonderful wife and mother and she deserves to be home with her family. Please, please let her go. Jen, if you can hear this, the kids and I love you and we're praying for you..."

"Yeah, that's short enough." *Any longer and North America is going to see a grown man blubbering his way through that.*

Tom was never one of those "macho" types, but he wasn't comfortable with letting anyone see him cry.

He also hated public speaking and remembered times in high school when he would get so nervous before giving a presentation in front of a group that his heart would begin to race and his palms would get sweaty. Of course, he didn't care about that now. He just wanted his wife and unborn baby returned home safely.

* * *

Little Buddy turned a roll inside Jenny as she sat quietly on the cot. As usual at this time of the morning, she was nauseated. It was mild, thank God, and she hadn't vomited since yesterday when she had awoken amidst this horrible nightmare.

She sat up and picked up the glass of water which sat on the small table beside the bed. As she held the glass to her lips, she shuddered. The water smelled like rotten eggs. She returned the glass to the table without taking a sip.

Despite the nausea, her stomach made noisy rumbling sounds. She turned her body to face the window. She didn't know what time it was, but surmised from the amount of light under the shade that it was probably mid-morning. *Tom, you must be so worried.*

*   *   *

Sergeant Romano arrived at the Callahan house and gave Tom an update on what she found on the cell phone and the lack of helpful information on the laptop computer. Neither of the revelations were a surprise. Tom knew that Jen used the cell phone and laptop infrequently. The cell phone was more or less for emergencies.

Tom introduced Sergeant Romano to Father Paul and they shook hands.

"Would it be permissible for Father Paul to introduce me at the press conference, Sergeant?"

"Certainly."

"Father Paul, Sergeant Romano, let me know what you think of my little speech."

"You've written it already?" Father Paul asked.

"Well, no. I have something composed in my mind."

"Tom?" Sergeant Romano asked.

"Yes?"

"Personalize Jenny. Allow the person who kidnapped her to see Jenny for the wonderful wife and mother she is."

He nodded. He began, "Please, whoever..." Tom bit down on his lip and lowered his head. Father Paul placed his hand on Tom's back and whispered, "Tom, are you sure you're ready for this?"

Tom turned to face the priest. "Father, if this will help find Jen, I'll do whatever it takes."

"All right. Go ahead."

Tom continued his soliloquy. When he finished, he took a deep breath. "I didn't think I was going to be able to do that without breaking up."

"You did great." Father Paul patted Tom's back.

"That sounds good," Sergeant Romano offered. "I'll go out and tell them you're coming out with a statement. Mrs.

Callahan, could you make sure the children stay inside?"

"Sure," the older woman answered.

Sergeant Romano opened the door to the shouts of the reporters. She closed it behind her and remained outside for several minutes before knocking. Then she waved her hand forward.

Father Paul then pushed the door open. Reporters shouted. Tom followed the priest, and on his way out, lifted the family portrait off the wall, the one with the identical outfits. Sergeant Romano motioned for the priest to step up toward the microphone, and accompanied Tom to an area just behind him.

"My name is Father Paul O'Neill and I'm a good friend of the Callahans. Mr. Callahan would like to give a short statement. Tom?" He stepped back, placed his hand on Tom's shoulder and led him to the microphone.

Tom gulped, and his heart began to race. He had no paper, no cheat sheet, no notes, just the photo, which he held up for everyone to see. He started to speak, then his voice cracked. He took a deep breath. Someone in the crowd coughed. He looked up.

"Yesterday, someone abducted my wife, Jennifer Callahan. She is nine months pregnant with our sixth child and is scheduled for a C-section in five days. She has a condition called placenta previa and will likely die if she does not deliver this baby by C-section. Please let her go. I beg you: Please, please let her come home. Do not harm her. She is a loving wife and a devoted mother. We love her so much. And Jen, if you can hear this, we're praying for your safe..." His voice began to crack again and he stopped. Taking a deep breath, he said, "We're praying for your safe return, Jen. I love you."

"Mr. Callahan, what will happen if your wife goes into labor before the scheduled C-section?"

"The placenta is almost completely covering the cervix. She needs to have this baby by C-section or she will die."

"Mr. Callahan, this kidnapping is being compared to the Laci Peterson kidnapping years ago. Can you comment?"

Tom clenched his fists and his jaw tightened at this reference to the infamous case of a husband convicted of murdering his pregnant wife and pretending that she had been abducted.   Father Paul whispered, "Are you okay, Tom? You don't have to answer that question."

"No," he whispered. "It's all right."

He straightened, took a deep breath and began, "The only aspect similar to that tragic case is that Laci Peterson was pregnant and Jen is pregnant. I did not harm my wife, nor would I ever harm her. And she will be found, I'm certain of that."

"Mr. Callahan..."

"No more questions," said Sergeant Romano as she pulled on Tom's arm. "The media relations officer will be giving a press conference at the station later on, once we have more information," she offered.

The priest took out his rosary. "If any of you in the media or neighbors want to participate, I welcome you to join me." He blessed himself. "For Jenny Callahan's safe return." Father Paul began to recite the rosary and some in the crowd soon responded as he led the prayers.

Fourteen

Denise watched the morning news conference with interest. Jenny's husband looked like he hadn't slept in weeks. But he appeared more attractive during the news conference than in the photo she had seen on the newscasts. Denise concluded that Tom must not be the photogenic sort. He was, however, quite well-spoken.

"Please, let her go. If she doesn't have a C-section…"

"Yeah, right, that's a ploy to get me to send Jenny back – no. I'm not going to fall for that," she said, speaking to the TV.

There's no way that's a real story. I've watched enough cop shows to know that's a ploy.

Denise chuckled. If, by some chance Jenny really did need a C-section, well, Denise would give it her best shot. She had decided not to tell Jenny that she was planning to kill her after the baby was born. The girl had behaved more calmly than she had thought she would. Denise was glad that she hadn't had to use the tranquilizers because it was better for the baby.

Listening to the rest of the news conference, she watched the priest say some prayers. Now disinterested, she turned the volume down. She hadn't gone to the bedroom yet with any kind of food, but she imagined that Jenny might be hungry. She checked the cupboards. She had already stocked it full of granola bars, crackers, and other supplies that would keep without refrigeration. The bar fridge in the cabin didn't hold much, and she didn't know how long she'd be here. She grabbed two granola bars, the chocolate chip kind, and some plain unsalted crackers.

* * *

Chris knew that her father was on the front lawn making some kind of speech to the reporters. Grandmom was keeping the kids in the kitchen so they couldn't see out the window.   She loved her grandmother, but sometimes, when she complained that Mom didn't clean well enough or that Mom didn't put an undershirt under Caleb's sweater, she didn't like that.

Nana would be coming soon. Chris would feel better when Nana came because Nana loved Mom so much.

She stood behind the closed drapes.   Father Paul sounded like he was saying a prayer. The large crowd was now responding to the prayers of the rosary. Chris remained behind the curtain and quietly joined in.

When the rosary was finished, she walked to the kitchen. She stared out the sliding glass doors that led to the backyard. There were two helicopters in the sky. She didn't like that so many people wanted to hear about her mom's kidnapping. She didn't like all the reporters on the front lawn. Chris felt useless. She wanted so much to help her mom but couldn't figure out how. Turning around, Chris stared at Grandmom and her little brother and sisters. Chloe was playing with her bowl of Rice Krispies more than eating them. Grandmom was feeding Caleb some oatmeal (even though he can feed himself) and the twins were talking to one another.

Jesus, please help my mom. Help them find my mom.

Across the kitchen and down the hallway adjacent to the living room, the front door opened then closed. Her dad and Father Paul and the tall lady cop were standing together. Then the lady cop walked into the kitchen and left Father Paul and Dad in the hallway. Dad leaned against the wall and whispered something to Father Paul, who nodded every few seconds. Dad then shook his head, and the two of them joined the lady cop in the kitchen.

Dad held his chin up higher than Chris could ever remember him holding it.   But she knew he was crying inside. She heard him last night sucking back air like he was going to cry. She wanted to tell him to go ahead and cry, that she would understand if he needed to.

Instead, she kept quiet.

"How did it go, Tom?" Grandmom asked.

"I suppose it went all right. Thanks for saying the rosary, Father Paul. I've been having a hard time praying." He took a seat next to her baby brother. "Hey, Caleb, your favorite oatmeal. Why is Grandmom feeding you?" He tried to smile as he said it and gently poked Caleb's arm.

"Come on, Tom. He makes such a mess. It's far easier to feed him than let him eat and spend time cleaning him up."

Dad pursed his mouth like he was annoyed, but trying to control himself. Father Paul stood behind Dad, but remained silent. Chris liked Father Paul because he always knew when to say something and when not to say something. And he was funny. He wasn't funny today. His eyes seemed sad. Of course, everyone's eyes seemed sad.

The sliding doors at the back opened, then closed and Aunt Patty came into the kitchen. Chris ran and hugged her favorite aunt. Aunt Patty had reddish brown hair and she was funny and loud and always brought presents for everyone. No presents today, though. Just hugs.

"Good idea to come in the back, Sis."

"I actually parked on MacDonald Street and I walked through someone else's backyard. Just a heads up, Tom. There are reporters back there. Someone might've followed me."

Dad nodded.

"You may want to ask one of the officers to take a position out back," Aunt Patty said.

Dad looked at the police officer in the corner. The cop smiled at Dad, then took out his cell phone and began talking on it.

"Most people are calling me, Tom, to ask if they can help. Jen's friend, Ginger, said that she's getting together a bunch of casseroles for you and the kids."

"That's great, thanks, Patty."

"Shelly and Amy want to know if there's anything they can do."

Chris didn't see Aunt Shelly and Aunt Amy, Dad's two older sisters, very much. They both lived far away. But Aunt Patty and Uncle Matt lived nearby and Chris was happy that she saw them a lot. They didn't have any kids yet.

"I've been getting a pestering phone call from a local television reporter asking for some video of Jen."

"What?"

"I kept hanging up on her, but then I thought about it. A video clip is better than a photo, Tom."

Dad didn't answer at first. Father Paul said, "It might be a good idea."

"I could take a bunch and go through them. Matt and I would be happy to do that for you."

"Go ahead. You know where we keep the videos and DVDs. The Christmas one is right up front. You can use that."

Aunt Patty hugged Dad. "All right. I've put an update on my Facebook page about Jen and I've already gotten many wall posts and messages...people inquiring how they can help."

Dad nodded.

Chris skirted past the group into the living room. Despite the distant chatter out front, it seemed still and quiet. The drapes were closed tight and the room was dark despite it being morning. Her eyes were drawn to the picture of Mary that Dad had given Mom for Christmas, a framed picture of "Our Lady of the Street," that hung over Mom's favorite chair, her nursing chair.

She turned to see Father Paul waving goodbye to everyone. "Call my cell if you need anything or if you hear anything. I'm heading over to the church. The ladies of the Catholic Women's League have set up round-the-clock adoration for Jenny's safe return, and I'm scheduled for the noon hour." Her dad nodded, then hugged Father Paul. She waved and he was gone. She could hear yelling out front, probably some of the reporters shouting questions. Chris decided that she didn't like reporters. They didn't really care about her mom. They didn't care that Mom liked pizza plain or that she hated fish or that she liked playing Barbies with her and her sisters. Those reporters only cared about the story.

Chris wanted so much to cry, but she had to keep it in. She didn't want her dad to have to comfort her when he had to deal with the little kids.

As her eyes welled up, she immediately wiped them dry. If she cried, her brother and sisters would cry too and she couldn't let that happen. She had to be a big girl and show Dad that she could be strong. But she missed Mom so much. If she had been willing to walk her sisters every day, then her mother wouldn't have had to come to the bus stop. Mom said she would be there early. Maybe that's why this happened. Her eyes began to water when she thought of how scared she had been when she had seen that weird woman staring at them from the window of the house across the street from the bus stop. She had looked back once and was positive that she saw that same lady on the opposite side of the street. That lady seriously creeped her out. *Wait a minute...that lady... could she have been the one that...*

"Daddy, Daddy, I think I saw who might have taken Mommy!

Fifteen

The door to the hot, stench-filled room opened, a warm waft of air drifted by Jenny as she was lying on her side facing away from the woman. She swung her legs over the side of the bed and struggled to sit up. Jenny avoided looking at her, but she felt the weight of her captor's eyes pressing down on her. Denise stood before her and threw some crackers and a granola bar onto the bed.

Jenny didn't want to admit it, but she was hungry and despite the fear, she thought that a granola bar and crackers sounded appetizing. She greedily took them, ripped off the packaging and ate them quickly.

Jenny swallowed the last bite of the granola bar, and made eye contact with her captor. "Why are you doing this? Please let me go. I just want to go home."

Denise stared at her and smiled. It was a weird sort of grimace and it made Jenny cringe.

"Please! Let me go home!"

She leaned in close to Jenny's face, the woman's sour breath hot and reeking of cigarettes. "I'm going to take your baby."

Jenny gasped. "What?"

"I'm taking your baby."

"You're crazy! This is my baby, not yours."

"Not anymore."

"No!" Jenny yelled.

"Look, the best thing you can do right now is calm down because you're gonna go into labor." Denise hesitated. "On second thought, perhaps that's a good idea. The sooner it happens, the sooner you can...uh...get back to your family. They must be very worried right now. Your husband looked like he was gonna cry at that press conference."

The thought of Tom on the verge of crying, the thought of him worrying made her heart ache. But this woman probably had no intention of taking Jenny back once she gave birth. She could see it in her eyes: no sympathy, no empathy, just selfishness. And actually, for a brief second, Jenny felt sorry for her.

"Your labor ought to be real quick. I've assisted many animals giving birth. I don't expect it will be all that much different."

"Home birth? You mean you expect me to just give birth..."

"You bet I do."

Just then, Jenny thought about the most recent complications of her pregnancy and why she was scheduled for a C-section. "Oh my God!"

"Praying won't help you now, Jenny."

"I've been diagnosed with..." Jenny stopped. Perhaps telling her that she had placenta previa would not be a good thing to do. She had no idea what that crazy woman would do with the information. Then again, maybe there was a trace of empathy left and she would set her free.

The woman frowned and responded, "Diagnosed with?"

"Nothing."

"You wanna know what I've been diagnosed with? Scarred fallopian tubes. I'll never have a baby. You, on the other hand just look at your husband and get pregnant."

Jenny shuddered at her last comment. Over the last couple of years, many people made fun of their having so many babies close together. She wanted to assure them that they did more than simply look at each other. Of course, after three heartbreaking miscarriages, Jenny, more than most people, understood the desire to have a baby. "What about adoption? My friend and her husband adopted two baby girls from China."

"Enough talking." She walked out the door.

Jenny let out a mournful sigh. *She's crazy. What if the placenta breaks away and I start to bleed? What will happen then?*

Jenny's heart began to pound and she held her lips together to stop herself from crying. Whatever that woman had in store for her, she had to hold out hope that this would end positively. She wouldn't give up now. It was important to remain strong for Tom and the kids. She lay her head down on the cot and took a few deep breaths.

She almost laughed out loud at the irony of it all. Last year, she had been angry with God after the last miscarriage. With determination, she pleaded with Tom to start trying to conceive right away rather than waiting a few months. She had never before been so grateful for their ease in getting pregnant because it happened immediately. She hoped this time would be different than the last three miscarriages, though. It *was* different, but for all the wrong reasons. The baby was still hanging on, but what would happen now? If this madwoman let her go into labor...or worse...no, Jenny couldn't think of that right now.

Shackled to the cot in the middle of who knows where, Jenny began to shake. How dare that woman talk about their fertility as if it were a commodity. After the last miscarriage, Jenny experienced days where the only thing that seemed to matter was that she get pregnant and stay pregnant. Losing a baby at any time in pregnancy was difficult, but the last time was at 20 weeks. The way she dealt with her grief was to immediately get pregnant again.

But to steal someone else's baby? That was lunacy.

Eleven years earlier

Jenny's heart began to pound in anticipation of seeing Tom as she walked down the laneway that led to his apartment in Kingston. Tom was enjoying his second year at university. It was a sunny but crisp late September Saturday morning.

She was feeling especially thankful that since Tom was so close while he went to university, they could see each other at least every other weekend. Her new job as a secretary at a local law firm meant that she wasn't free during the week, but weekends were wide open for visits. Last year, it had been difficult getting accustomed to not seeing him every day, but they spoke on the phone most days. Tom had email, but Jenny's mom didn't have a computer so the only time she could communicate that way was from the law firm.

Jenny buzzed Tom's apartment. As she waited the few seconds for him to buzz back, she reveled in the cool autumn air and the beautiful red and orange leaves on the trees besides the doorway. The intercom buzzed back. Jenny smiled. "Come on up, Jen," sounded like Scooby Doo saying, "Rom up, Ren..."

Jenny climbed the steps. At the doorway to his floor, he met her in an embrace. They hugged for a few seconds. "Jen, I missed you so much." He took her by the hand and escorted her into his apartment, closing the door. They kissed.

"Yeah, I missed you too, Tom."

"Where's your roommate?" she said, pulling away from him.

"Away for the weekend. We've got this place to ourselves all day."

"Oh, we do, do we?"

"We do."

Tom reached for his jacket. "Let's go to my favorite restaurant for breakfast."

"Please, Tom, don't make me eat there."

"They've got a two for one Egg McMuffin deal on, Jen."

"That stuff's not good for you. I'd like us to have a nice long happy life together."

"We will. Come on." Tom was using his puppy dog eyes to get what he wanted. He was good at it and she always gave in. "All right."

"Besides, we can stop at the video store in the mall and rent a couple of movies to watch later on."

"*I have to leave by four. My mom needs the car by seven.*"

"*You mean you won't be able to stay for the game tonight? I'm the starting quarterback again.*"

"*Sorry, Tom.*"

"*That's okay.*"

"*I miss going to Mass with you.*"

"*Uh...right.*" Tom walked alongside her to his car. When she said something about Mass, he seemed to flinch. "*Tom, you are still going to Mass, aren't you?*"

"*Uh...well... sometimes.*"

"*What do you mean sometimes?*"

"*Well, to be honest, I haven't been going to Mass.*"

"*Tom.*" She sighed. "*Before we go to breakfast, you should find someplace to go to Confession.*"

"*It's just been so busy here, my course load is tough this year.*"

"*All the more reason to go to Confession and Mass.*"

"*Come on, Jen. I'll go later.*"

"*All right,*" she said, convincing herself that he would.

*   *   *

Later they returned to the apartment and Tom stood beside the television, holding up the two videos. "*Which one do you want to watch first, Message in a Bottle or The Blair Witch Project?*"

Her mouth turned into a thin line, her eyebrows narrowed as she stared at the two cases. "*Message in a Bottle. It's too early to watch a scary movie.*"

"*Somehow I knew you'd choose that one.*"

They sat on the couch and Tom reached over her to get two throw pillows and propped them against the arm of the couch. He leaned on them and pulled her close.

She relaxed against him. Ten minutes into the movie, however, she heard Tom snoring. She chuckled under her breath, but tried to remain still so she wouldn't disturb him.

Being with him while he was asleep was better than not being with him at all.

Tom's even breathing caused Jenny to close her eyes a short time later.

The ending credits began to play and Jenny sat upright. Tom roused enough to say, "Uh-oh, did I fall asleep?"

"Uh-huh. I did too."

He stretched, then pulled her close to him and kissed the top of her head. Jenny always felt safe and fulfilled in Tom's arms. They lay still, then Tom trailed a line of kisses from her forehead to her nose, to her lips. She caressed the back of his neck. She had yearned to be with Tom all week and now that she was here, alone with him, she wanted nothing more than to mold herself to him. As they continued kissing, time seemed to stop. His smell, his breathing, his moaning pushed her to the point of no return. Tom was now on top of her, kissing her face, her neck. She heard the sound of his zipper and, for a second, she thought, "No." But all she could think about was that she loved Tom with all her heart, with all her soul and with all her body. Pushing her conscience aside, she gave in to the moment of passion. All her thoughts, hopes and feelings were now wrapped in his arms.

Afterwards, they lay still together. Now that it was over, Jenny was frightened. She felt like they had spoiled a beautiful moment that was meant to be enjoyed and treasured after they had gotten married.

Jenny couldn't speak. Instead, she wept.

"Jen, I'm so sorry. I...shouldn't have...we shouldn't have..."

Tom began to kiss her tears as they ran down her face.

Jenny gasped as Little Buddy kicked her in the ribs.

Then, with a groan, she realized that she would have to pee again in the pail. She stumbled across the room – the shackles allowed just enough travel space to make it to the pail – relieved herself, then plopped back on the already soiled bed. The room smelled like an outhouse. *Even if I wasn't pregnant, I'd want to throw up.* Although she had eaten two granola bars and a few crackers, Jenny's stomach was now calling out for more food. At least she had some water on the bedside table and she now took a long drink in. It smelled of sulfur, which was a good indication of what the rest of the room smelled like.

Please, God, help me. My family must be so worried.

She wondered whether the local news carried information about her being missing. Her initial thought was *I hope the authorities don't use my driver's license photo.* She had been pregnant with Caleb and had a bloated face. But on top of that, she wasn't smiling so the photo was worse than a typical mug shot. "If I ever go missing," she teased Tom, "Don't ever let the police use this photo." "Why would I?" he answered, "They'd never recognize you from this photo." Now, in retrospect, that whole conversation seemed ludicrous. In actuality, she couldn't care less about what photo they used. She just wanted to be found — or have a chance to escape — and to return home.

Home. She missed Tom and the kids so much. Her eyes began to water when she thought of Tom's reaction to her discomfort about her body after Caleb was born. She had gained a whopping 60 pounds, much of it in her stomach.

Tom caressed her arm and began to slip off her shirt.
Jenny pulled away.
"What's the matter, Hon?"
"I just had a baby and I look so...fat."
"You look great."
"Liar."
"I am not a liar. You do look great."

Jen then lifted her shirt and said, "This looks great, this three inches of fat around my middle, yeah, right." She grasped onto the flab with both hands.

Tom responded by gazing at her as if she was the most beautiful woman in the world.

Jenny began to sob. Tom had a remarkable talent for making her feel like the most beautiful, desirable woman in the world, despite her imperfections, despite the extra weight she had gained. Tom was such a wonderful man and how blessed she was to have found him so early in her life. They had built a beautiful, happy life together.

She had only been away from her family for 24 hours and yet it seemed like an eternity. Only five days to go before she was scheduled to have a C-section, but Jenny couldn't think of that right now. She knew that she would have to focus on keeping herself and Little Buddy alive.

Sixteen

Tom and his sister rushed into the living room where his daughter screamed for him.

"Daddy, remember two days ago when Mommy fell asleep and didn't meet us at the bus stop?"

"Yes."

"I saw a lady. She was standing at the window in the house across the street from the bus stop and she was staring at us."

"Just because you..."

"Wait, wait. She was big, tall and had dark hair and she was smoking a cigarette."

"Chris, people are allowed to look out from their windows."

"Daddy, you don't understand. She must have come out of her house, because I'm sure I saw her on the other side of the street when we were walking home. Can't you call the lady cop? I can tell her what she looked like. I think I remember seeing her at the vet's office when we took Bootsie there."

"Okay, honey." Tom wasn't sure the information was relevant. Statistically speaking, the chances of this particular woman having something to do with Jen's kidnapping were probably slim to none, but he decided that any information was better than none. Tom reached for the phone and dialed Sergeant Romano's BlackBerry number. She answered on the second ring.

"Sergeant Romano."

"Yes, this is Tom Callahan."

"Yes, Tom. Is everything all right?"

"Yes. My oldest daughter thinks she might have some helpful information."

"I'll be right over."

Tom hung up the phone. "She said she'll be right over.

Patty, can you take the kids into the kitchen? Mom has lunch prepared."

"Sure, Tom."

Tom parted the drapes at the front window. There had to be over a hundred reporters and cameramen on his small lawn. Someone clearing his throat behind him made Tom turned around. Jeff Anderson stood before him.

"Tom?"

"Yes?"

"I...uh... wanted to...well, what I'm trying to say is...I wanted to apologize, you know, for the stupid way I acted in high school. It...it was pretty bad."

"Bad? You humiliated Jenny."

"I know. I was an idiot and a jerk."

"You can say that again."

"I just wanted you to know something." Jeff paused and lowered his head. Then he made eye contact. "Eight years ago, I accepted Jesus Christ as my Lord and Savior and my life has never been the same. My wife and I both are praying for Jenny. I don't know what I'd do if this happened to me. You're holding up extremely well."

Tom nodded, then faced the curtained window. He heard Jeff leave the room. He listened to the chattering of the people outside, like this was just another reporting day, and the familial murmuring in the kitchen, his mom's controlling tone of voice, Patty's high-pitched speech when talking to the children. It felt like an immense rock of helplessness had taken up residence in the middle of his chest, and was now making its way to his throat. He parted the curtains and stared at the reporters outside. *She isn't just another story. She's a real person.*

Please God, keep her safe.

* * *

At the Sutherland OPP Detachment, Kathy closed her laptop. "We're going to the Callahan residence," she said to Bob Preston. She grabbed her coffee and headed to the car.

Caffeine and adrenaline were the only things keeping her awake. Although she attempted to sleep last night, she only managed to rest for about two hours.

In the car, Kathy sat in the passenger seat while Bob drove. Bob remained quiet. Her mind was a jumble of a hundred different scenarios. Did the kidnapper take Jenny far away or could she still be in town? She couldn't rule out either of those yet. Although she had never worked on a case like this, she suspected that the perpetrator was an infertile woman.

She tried to put herself in the mind of a woman who was desperate to have a child. Kathy smiled inwardly. Admittedly, it wasn't hard to empathize with infertile women. Fourteen years ago, in the moments after she gave birth to her son, the doctors had had to perform an emergency hysterectomy because of complications. She was disappointed, even depressed, for weeks. Instead of dwelling on her misfortune, however, she eventually decided that she would look ahead and focus on her career. As it happened, she was able to advance to the position of Area Crime Sergeant, a position she truly loved.

At the Callahan house, Kathy and Bob maneuvered their way through the crowd of reporters waiting in front. She knocked a few times. Tom opened the door and ushered them in. As he was closing it, several reporters shouted questions, but he ignored them.

"Thank you for coming, Sergeant, Constable." Chris stood behind her father in the front entryway. Kathy smiled awkwardly and was surprised when she returned a slight smile.

"Why don't we go into the kitchen with your dad?"

"Okay."

Tom, Chris and Kathy sat at the kitchen table. Bob Preston stood beside the table and took notes. Doris asked the two officers if they would like some coffee.

Bob smiled and shook his head.

Kathy needed more caffeine. "Yes, black, please." Then, looking at the little girl, she said, "Can you describe the woman you saw the other day, Christine?"

"She had short brown hair, was shorter than my mom, was chunky and was smoking a cigarette. I remember thinking that I was glad I wasn't near her because I don't like cigarettes."

"Where was she?"

"She was in the house across from the bus stop and looking at us through the window."

"Directly across from the bus stop?"

"Uh-huh."

"Can you remember anything else, honey?" Tom asked.

"Do you think she had something to do with my mom's disappearance?"

"I'm not sure," Kathy said.

"But she really creeped me out."

"Creeped you out? Why?"

"After I saw her looking at us through her window, we were walking home, I looked back and saw her on the other side of the street. When I looked back again, she was gone."

"What was she wearing, Christine?"

"Dark clothes, I think maybe jeans and a sweatshirt."

"That's good. You can go ahead into the living room and watch television."

Chris nodded and began to walk away, then turned around. "This lady, I knew I had seen her once before, but I couldn't remember at first. Now I know where I've seen her. She works at the vet's office."

"Do you remember the name of the vet's office?"

"I think it's called the Sutherland Veterinary Hospital."

"Thank you, Christine. That was extremely helpful." The little girl gazed at her with an expression of relief. She was so young but seemed to carry so heavy a burden, as if everyone was depending on her to find her mom.

Kathy turned toward Tom. "Is that the name of the vet's office that you use?"

"I'd have to look it up. Jen usually takes Bootsie in for her shots, but there are only two here, the Sutherland Veterinary Hospital and the Main Street Animal Hospital."

"Thanks, Tom. I'll get on this right away."

Seventeen

All the major news channels were covering Jenny's disappearance, screaming out to her that Jenny would die if she wasn't brought home immediately and allowed to have a C-section. *Placenta previa. Placenta previa. Jenny Callahan will die.* Tom Callahan was telling the truth. This was no ploy.

When Denise was initially planning this, she thought perhaps that she would simply kidnap Jenny, take her baby, then let her go. But she realized that for this whole plan to work, she would have to kill Jenny after she gave birth. It was a necessary killing, just like when the fertility doctor explained to her and Lou that many embryos created for in-vitro are destroyed in order to implant only the most promising ones. She didn't really want Jenny searching for her child and she figured that her husband would be too racked with grief and busy taking care of five kids to concern himself with that.

But in all her research, it never occurred to her to find out if there was something actually wrong with Jenny's current pregnancy. Since she was planning to kill her after the birth, it didn't matter how she died. She was perfectly prepared to take the baby regardless.

Denise turned up the volume on the television set. A doctor was describing what placenta previa was and showing an illustration of what could happen if the mother went into labor.

The doctor on the television said that the baby could also die from oxygen deprivation if the placenta came away from the uterine wall. She pounded the chair with her fists. Denise had not orchestrated this entire thing to lose that baby now. "Damn it, damn it!" she screamed and pitched the remote control across the room.

* * *

Jenny's eyes flew open. Denise was swearing. Thump. It sounded like something hard had hit the other side of the wall. She swung her legs over the bed and pushed herself into a sitting position. The door banged open. Jenny turned and tried to face her as she entered.

"You have placenta previa."

"Yes," Jenny whispered. What else could she say to this woman?

"Yeah, well, either way, I'm taking the baby."

"I could bleed to death before he's even born. And if I die, my baby dies."

"I'm already in too deep. I'm not backing out now."

"Please, I know that you want a baby, but this isn't your baby to have. This baby that you want so desperately would only be yours because I died."

Denise seemed to be considering Jenny's words. She scowled, then slammed the palm of her hand onto the small table. Jenny jumped back.

"I don't care," she said, quietly at first. Then, with each word, she became louder. "I'm in this too deep," she said, her voice now pitched, "and so are you. I...am taking the...baby." Jenny kept silent, but held her hand protectively over her abdomen.

Her captor leaned in close to her, "Do you hear me?" Jenny shrunk back away from the woman's hot breath and avoided eye contact. Jenny refused to answer because she would never, ever give her baby to this woman.

Looking up, Jenny shuddered at Denise's rage-filled expression. She blurted out, "Why are you so angry? I've never done anything to you."

"Oh, really? You and all the other women in the world who get pregnant at the mere thought. You strut around with your big stomachs like you're part of some special club."

Jenny cringed but kept silent. Special club? How could she tell her that in many respects she understood her? Why did people automatically assume that just because she had five children, that she had never had any problems?

The woman kicked the side of the cot. Jenny kept her head lowered, staring at her captor's running shoes. Jenny tried to remain calm, but her heart was pounding and her whole body began to shake.

"You see, Jenny, it all makes perfect sense, doesn't it?" she shot at her, small amounts of spit spraying Jenny's face.

"God, please," Jenny muttered, her eyes facing the floor.

"God never helped me. So I decided to help myself and take your baby."

Denise finally stopped talking. A minute, then two minutes passed by, with both women awkwardly remaining quiet. From the other room, the newscaster mentioned a "press conference."

Immediately, Denise rushed out of the room, excitement pitching her voice. "Your husband's going to talk to the reporters again. I'll turn it up nice and loud so you can hear it this time."

Eighteen

Tom felt like a prisoner in his own home. It didn't feel like it was his home anymore with his mother there, Jeff Anderson on duty — he supposed to babysit the family and/or house — several other OPP officers and dozens of media out front. Sergeant Romano had just returned to be present when he ventured outside to talk to reporters again.

Of course, he really couldn't leave his house because reporters would follow him, like they had done with his sister, Patty, earlier today, despite the fact that she had left via the back door. She'd called from her cell phone to say that a few trucks had followed her home. His brother-in-law, Matt, had shouted a few unkind words to the reporters and they'd finally left.

Tom could see that his kids were engrossed in a DVD, except Chris, who rarely left his side and who now stood beside him near the window.

His dad was scheduled to arrive any minute with Jen's mom, Susan. Her plane had been an hour late. It had been sitting on the ground in Winnipeg because of heavy rains and a thunderstorm. On top of that, he would have to deal with the tension that always filled the air whenever his parents were in the same house...as if there wasn't already enough tension in the room. Now, most especially, he had zero patience for their attitude toward one another. He would not tolerate their animosity when his wife and unborn child were missing.

He studied his daughter, who was peeking outside at the crowd on the lawn. He crouched down. "Are you all right, Chris?"

She looked up with tear-filled eyes. "I'm scared for Mommy. I miss her so much." She wiped her eyes.

"I'm scared for Mommy too."

"Do you think that lady cop will be able to find

Mommy? Did that lady take Mommy?"

"I don't know. But I do know, if that lady did take Mommy, Sergeant Romano and the OPP will do everything they can to find her."

He pulled his daughter into his arms. She hugged him tight, then backed away and straightened. "I'm okay, Daddy."

He knew that his daughter kept her tears at bay for him, but he wanted to tell her that if she needed to cry, it would be fine. But he felt like he couldn't say that now, because he didn't know whether it would be fine and he didn't want to lie to her.

Sergeant Romano motioned for Tom to join him in the kitchen. "Tom, it's time to give another press conference."

"I'll be out in a few minutes."

Tom positioned himself behind Sergeant Romano. He wished that he could crawl into a hole, but he knew it was essential for him to remain strong for Jen and for the kids. But what if Jen didn't come back? What if the person or persons had already harmed her? He didn't want to even consider that she might be suffering, and he certainly couldn't imagine his life without her.

He followed Sergeant Romano to the front lawn, and gazed into the faceless crowd as he stood before the microphone. There had to be over 100 reporters and spectators on his small front lawn and spilling onto the street, each one wanting a story or curious enough to watch.

"I'm here again to plead for the safe return of my beautiful wife, Jenny, and our unborn baby. Please, whoever has Jen, bring her home. She may die if she does not have a C-section. Our children need her. I need her. She will...I can't live without her..." His voice began to crack. "Please, please, bring Jen...home." He backed away and rushed into the house.

Nineteen

From the room where she was being held captive, Jenny heard the emotion in Tom's voice. Her heart felt heavy and a sob crept up the back of her throat. "I'm here, Tom."

How could she possibly escape this situation? After all that she had been through with this pregnancy, she would not, could not, give up. Again, she searched the room with her eyes: one blind-covered window, a small table at her bedside, a metal pail, but no furniture other than the cot. What if she tried to hurt her captor when she came in the room? She sank back against the cot. If she attempted anything of that nature, if she flung herself at Denise, perhaps the baby's condition might be compromised. She couldn't risk her child being harmed in any way.

Hearing her strong husband's voice filled with emotion, Jenny wanted so much to embrace him, to tell him that everything would be all right.

Eleven years earlier

Jenny drove up in front of Tom's apartment and sat in the car for over an hour. No matter how hard she tried, she couldn't think of the right words. "I'm pregnant," seemed too clinical. "We're going to have a baby, sweetheart" seemed too jovial for the situation. "I'm knocked up," sounded like Rizzo from the movie Grease.

Last week, her period had been one week late. Month after month, Jenny had always dreaded the first day of her cycle. Now, she found herself begging for the relief it would bring her. When she'd taken a pregnancy test and the telltale extra blue line had shown up, she'd taken another, then another. She had to drive all the way to Fraser to buy the tests because she didn't want anyone she knew to see her buying them. At a whopping 14 bucks apiece, they sucked most of her spending money for the week. In their phone conversations these past few days, Jenny had been quiet and Tom had asked why. She had said that she was tired; she couldn't yet tell him, not on the phone anyway.

Three tests later — all showing positive results — a missed period and nausea seemed to be all the information she needed. It was now time to tell Tom. How would he react? Since that night four weeks ago, he'd seemed steadfastly committed to never letting "that" happen again until they got married. He even went to confession with her and promised that he would begin attending Mass.

She still couldn't believe that they had actually done it. In hindsight, she wondered whether it had just been a matter of time. Earlier in their relationship, they had only kissed, but over the past year or so, kissing had slowly progressed to touching...that, coupled with the weeks spent apart, the time alone, the falling asleep. Oh well. They couldn't change what they had done now. But what would they do? Jenny thought of the different possibilities. They had already talked about getting married, but Tom still had two years left before he finished his accounting degree. She would have to find a job here on campus or close to Kingston and their baby would have to be in day care. Jenny was sure that Tom would not encourage her to have an abortion. Give the baby up for adoption? It seemed like the only rational solution right now, but how could she ever give up this baby, the fruit of their love? Jenny thought of her own biological parents. Did her birth mother have this same awkward reckoning as she tried to figure out a solution?

Finally, Jenny got out of the car. She hesitated at the doorway to Tom's apartment building. She stared at the intercom system just inside the door. Normally Tom was either there to let her in or upstairs in his room waiting for her. This morning, he had no idea that she was coming this early, so he was probably still asleep. She waited in the foyer, staring at the intercom system, tapping her foot as she thought about what to do.   Within a few moments, Jenny saw one of the tenants out of the corner of her eye, who recognized her with a smile and let her in.

She took the stairs up to the third floor, and slowly crept down the hall. She had to step over several beer cans and other debris left over, no doubt, from a student's party the previous night. All seemed quiet now and it would, since it was only eight o'clock in the morning. She knew that Tom wouldn't be expecting her until noon, but she couldn't wait any longer. Holding this secret inside at times during the past week Jenny had thought she was going to explode. She hadn't planned on telling anyone yet, but the last time she spoke with her friend, Ginger, she couldn't help it. It just came out. Ginger urged her to tell Tom. Jenny didn't want to break her mother's heart yet, so she promised herself and Ginger that she would share the news with Tom at the first opportunity. Now.

Standing before his doorway, she took a deep breath and let it out slowly. Jenny stretched out her hand to knock, but noticed her hand was shaking. She pulled it back, holding her palm protectively against her chest. She waited a few moments, then knocked quietly. Not hearing any response, she pounded more heavily. Tom's roommate opened the door. He was squinting and his black hair was messed. He was dressed in long pajama pants and no shirt. "What is it?"

"Hi, Sam. Can I speak to Tom?"

She could hear Tom behind the door, "Jen?" Sam stepped aside and stumbled back into his room as Tom came to the door. Like Sam, he was squinting and his red hair had definite 'bed head.' He was pulling his robe on.

"What's the matter, Hon? Everything okay?"

She shook her head. "We need...to talk."

"Yeah, yeah, sure thing. Just give me a minute and I'll get some clothes on." Jenny took off her coat and waited in the living room for what seemed like an hour, although it

was probably no more than a minute. Tom came out of his room dressed in jeans and a brown sweater. He pulled her into an embrace.

"Gosh, I missed you so much, Jen. I'm glad you're here." She responded by hugging him so hard that he asked, "What's wrong?" Jenny knew that he would fix this and whatever he decided would be the right choice. He made things better. He was good at that.

As much as she tried not to, she began to sob. "Oh, Tom."

"Hey, hey, whatever it is, it's going to be fine." He sat her down on the plaid couch and wiped away her tears with his thumbs. He kissed her forehead. "Is your mom all right?"

She nodded.

"Then what's wrong?"

At first, she stared at him but kept silent. Then she whispered, "I'm...we're..."

Without hearing anything further, he seemed to know. "Oh, no." He lowered his head. "Have you been to a doctor?"

"No, but I took three tests. They're all positive."

He let out a long sigh. Then Tom, the master of problem solving, the hero who had rescued her from the bullies two years ago, began to weep.

Twenty

Kathy drove into the parking lot of the Sutherland Veterinary Hospital. Bob offered, "I think my wife takes our cat to this place." Kathy nodded.

Since she worked so many hours and since she and her husband weren't animal people, Kathy never had any reason to visit a vet's office, except for professional reasons. Even though her son had begged her to get a dog, she and her husband had remained steadfast.

As she and Bob approached the building, a large ranch style house converted into a vet clinic, she noticed storm clouds gathering in the distance.

Inside, several people sat on the chairs and their dogs barked impatiently. Sergeant Romano approached the reception desk. "Excuse me?" she said to the woman behind the desk whose name tag identified her as Sherry. Kathy flashed her badge. "I'm Area Crime Sergeant Kathy Romano and this is Constable Preston from the Sutherland OPP Detachment. We'd like to ask some questions regarding an employee of yours, Denise Kramer?"

"Sure. What would you like to know?"

"We'd like to speak to Dr. Eastman as well."

"Certainly." The phone rang. "Excuse me." Sherry answered the phone, spoke for a minute, then hung up. "Sorry. It's been a zoo in here, literally. We had a few emergencies, one dog hit by a car, another hit by a paint ball in the eye."

"Yes, I realize it's busy in here but we're investigating the disappearance of Jenny Callahan."

"Oh, yes. Bootsie is a patient here. We all love Bootsie. She's so..."

Kathy cut her off. "I'm sorry to interrupt, but we need to ask a few questions about Denise Kramer. Is Dr. Eastman or another supervisor here?"

The phone rang again. Kathy sighed as Sherry picked it up.

"Perhaps you should take us to Dr. Eastman?"

Sherry held her finger up to indicate she'd only be a minute. Kathy had to control her urge to yank the phone away from her. The receptionist finally hung up and faced the officers. "I'm sorry. Now what did you want to know?"

"Could we see Dr. Eastman?"

"Yes, of course."

The phone rang again, but this time, Sherry ran off to the back. The dogs in the waiting room continued to bark. Sherry waved to the two officers to proceed to the back. She pointed them to an examining room where Dr. Eastman, a short middle-aged woman with light brown hair, was writing on a clipboard.

The veterinarian looked up and smiled. "I'm Dr. Eastman. What can I do to help?"

"My name is Sergeant Romano and this is OPP Constable Bob Preston. We'd like to ask you some questions about your employee, Denise Kramer."

"Certainly. Denise is on maternity leave. Three weeks ago she asked to take her leave early since she was having some problems."

"Did she say what sort of problems?"

"No, actually, she was vague most of the time, except when she told us about the pregnancy. She seemed to talk non stop for weeks about it. Other than that, she never shared much about her personal life, at least not with me. To be honest, I was eager for her to take maternity leave early, so I readily agreed. In fact, I had just returned from a short maternity leave myself."

"Congratulations."

"Thank you. He's my first and, likely, my only. I probably shouldn't have waited so long to have a baby, but other things seemed more important when I was younger. My husband and I were fortunate."

"So why were you eager for her to leave?"

"Denise is a good vet tech, but easily distracted. And there's something "not right" about her. Sometimes she's very happy, almost to an extreme, and other times, depressed and sullen. Before she became pregnant, I was considering letting her go. I couldn't do it once she told me she was pregnant."

"Did Denise say how she became pregnant? She's divorced."

"Yes. She said she got pregnant through in vitro fertilization."

"One more question. Would Denise have ever assisted in animal surgeries?"

"Yes. But again, I avoided assigning her surgeries because of her mood swings."

"Have you noticed any drugs missing?"

"To be honest, there are some medications missing. From my cursory check of the books since I've returned, I've noticed Diazepam, Ketamine and Sleepaway are missing. I'm not so worried about the Diazepam and Ketamine, because those are spilled or wasted on a regular basis. But the euthanasia drug, that shouldn't be missing. Unfortunately, the person I employed to take my place didn't do much in the way of inventory, but I'll be rectifying that situation in the coming weeks and performing a more detailed investigation."

"Thank you, Doctor, you've been extremely helpful."

"Sergeant?"

"Yes."

"Does this have to do with the missing pregnant woman?"

"All we can say is that Denise is a person of interest."

"I hope that you find Jenny. She's a sweet girl. I've always admired her for the patience she shows with her children."

"Thanks. Oh, and Doctor?"

"Yes?"

"Please do not speak to anyone about this."

"Of course."

On the way back to the car, her cell rang. The RCMP matched one of the partial prints on Jenny's cell phone to none other than Denise Kramer, who was in the system for driving while under the influence.

In the patrol car, Kathy turned to Bob. "If Denise was pregnant, why would she take Jenny?"

"Maybe she lost the baby."

"Or perhaps she wasn't pregnant to begin with."

Twenty-One

Jenny laid her head on the meager, flat pillow. She was afraid to close her eyes, despite her fatigue, but had allowed herself five-minute cat naps. Even during the night, she tossed and turned. Hunger, fear, uncertainty — not to mention being nine months pregnant — kept her from slipping too deeply into sleep.

God, please help me make it out of this situation alive. Guardian Angel, protect me and Little Buddy.

During her last miscarriage, she had begged God to spare her baby. When she had started bleeding, she had recited rosary after rosary and said prayers to every saint she could think of. Then, with each gush of blood, her hope vanished, until she stopped begging God and let it happen. All the begging and pleading with God during this pregnancy, even during her last bleeding episode a month ago, and this is where it landed her: right into the arms of a crazy kidnapper. Her attitude softened. This wasn't God's fault.

Her back was toward the door as she heard it open. She kept her eyes closed and her breathing steady. Footsteps approached.

"Jenny!" Denise's piercing voice made Jenny cringe.

"What do you want?" Jenny answered, as she opened her eyes, pulled herself up on the bed, and faced her captor, who dropped another TV dinner onto the bed side table, then scowled at Jenny.

"Please, I beg you. Let me go home. I won't tell anybody about you."

"I already told you. You're not going home. You need to focus on having that baby."

"I could die."

The woman snorted and laughed at the same time. Jenny had to choke back a sob.

"Look, there's no need to pretend anymore. You *are* going to die."

Jenny gasped. The horrid woman said it as if she were telling Jenny that she was taking a walk around the block or announcing the weather report.

"Please, I have small children who need me!" Jenny's voice was cracking as she pleaded.

"Yeah, well, they have a father who can care for them."

"But they need their mother too."

"I already told you. I'm in this too deep. I'm here for your baby. If you start bleeding, I may just have to take him from you. But don't worry. I'll put you out first. I've got some medicine for that. Now, do you want this TV dinner or not?"

Jenny turned away. Her stomach felt like one large knot. Finally, she shook her head.

*   *   *

Denise left the room and plopped the TV dinner on the tray in front of her. She'd been hoping that Jenny wouldn't want it because she really liked turkey. She would have had to make another one in the microwave. She savored the food, continuing to watch the news. She took the last swig of root beer and reached into her purse for her cigarettes. She pulled it out to discover there weren't any left in the package, then her eyes scanned the room. Where did she put that other pack of cigarettes?

She dumped her purse onto the floor, no cigarettes. She swung the cupboards wide open and peered inside. She pulled drawers open. No cigarettes, save for a few butts in the ashtray.

She refused to spend the next few days with no cigarettes. Besides, she needed to get out of the stuffy cottage for a while. This seemed as good a time as any to drive down the road to pick up some extra provisions at the convenience store.

Twenty-Two

Chris anxiously waited by the side door. Dad told her that Grandpop and Nana would be arriving from the airport at any minute. He'd told them to use the side door because there were fewer reporters there.

She had really missed Nana, especially in the last day or so since Mom had been gone. Chris and Nana had a special bond, not only because she was the oldest grandchild, but because they shared the same birthday, June 2nd. Mom used to tell her that when Chris was in her tummy, Nana kept saying that the baby would be born on her birthday. She was right. Of course, Nana was always right.

"They're here, they're here," the twins squealed. Callie and Cassie ran past Chris and stood in front of her as they anxiously watched the door open.

"Nanny, Nanny!" Callie and Cassie cried. Nana crouched down and hugged both girls. Chris moved aside to allow her younger brother and sister to gather around their grandmother.

"Chris, how are you doing?" Nana gave her a hug. Chris was nearly as tall as her grandmother and responded by tightly returning the embrace. Nana put her arm around Chris's shoulder and walked into the kitchen.

"I'll be on my way," Grandpop said to her dad. Chris turned and stared at her grandfather. He never stayed long if Grandmom was around. Chris was sad that she couldn't visit them together anymore.

Chris liked spending time with Nana. Nana always wore jeans and she usually smiled a lot. Nana wasn't smiling now. Instead, her eyes looked sad. Nana hugged Dad for a long time.

Finally, Nana spoke up.

"Tom, I'm worried sick about her."

"Me too."

"Any news or leads?"

"Not much."

Did her father forget about the lady she told him about? Even the lady cop thought it might be important. "What about the lady, Dad? What about the lady I saw?"

Her dad smiled, like he was humoring her. "Oh, right. Chris says she saw a woman staring at the girls the other day from the house across from the bus stop. The police are doing everything they can. And there's been no ransom demand."

"Well, Tom, you never know. That woman may have something to do with this." Nana glanced at Chris and nodded.

"It's a long shot, though. And I hate the fact that there are so many news vans outside our door."

"The more people who know, the more chance there is that someone might see something. This is a good thing that the news trucks are there."

Chris didn't know whether to agree with Nana. She didn't like all the trucks. Most importantly, she didn't like that Mom was gone and maybe hurt somewhere and there was nothing that Chris could do. Nothing, except pray. She looked up again at the crucifix and the picture of Our Lady next to it. *Please, Jesus and Mary, keep my mom safe.*

* * *

"Where are you going with that laundry, Mom?" Tom asked, as he watched his mother open the door to the basement.

"To wash it."

The basement was always the messiest room in their house. With the heavy rains last week, they had some water in the basement and he had not cleaned it up yet. His mother would be the last person Jen would want to see the mess.

"No, I'll take it down."

Doris stared at him with eyebrows raised, then snorted

and handed the basket to him. Tom knew that his mom
didn't approve of him doing the laundry or any tasks
supposedly meant to be done by a woman. During his teen
years, his chores always involved taking out the trash or
mowing the lawn. Never was he asked to do laundry or
dishes or cleaning. Those were always taken care of by his
sisters or their mom.

And now, despite the fact that Jen was missing and
God-knows-where, all of the day-to-day chores still had to be
completed. As much as he hated it, the world went on.

Tom trudged down the basement steps to the washer
and dryer. He was thankful for something to do. He
desperately needed to be alone. The only time he had spent
by himself in the past 24 hours was when he went to the
bathroom.

Checking the washer, he discovered a load mostly of his
underwear and socks that Jenny must have done yesterday
morning. He cringed as he thought of how he spoke so
sharply with her and he wished that he could go back in time
and take it back. She didn't deserve to be the brunt of his
frustration and anger.

He lifted the clothes out of the washer and threw them
into the dryer and turned it on. Immediately, he was struck
by the normalcy of Jen throwing a bunch of clothes in the
washer. Of him going off to work. The kids leaving for
school. Normal. Would their routine ever be normal again?

Methodically, he took the clothes out of the basket and
stuffed them into the washer. He knew that he ought to
separate the whites from the darker clothes, but decided
against it. Most of these clothes were in no danger of
bleeding their color.

He poured the detergent in, then set the machine and
watched it fill. He had so much pent-up anxiety, frustration
and worry; he needed to find a way to release it without
becoming hysterical. Eyeing the treadmill, he walked over to
it and turned it on. He started out slow, but increased the

speed every minute or so. Finally, he was running. His body was now sweating minute tears; his eyes joined along. He stopped the machine, wiped his eyes and made his way over to the dryer. He listened to the hum of the dryer, a soothing sound.

Not knowing was the worst part of this horrible experience. *Oh, Jen, please be all right. I can't stand the thought of you suffering.* "I love you, Jen. Keep strong," he said out loud.

Small droplets from his eyes fell onto the surface of the warm appliance. He always tried to remain strong, because that's what his dad taught him. No matter what, a man stays strong and in control.

Eleven years earlier

"This is my fault that you're pregnant, Jen. I should've been in control. Your mom trusted me. You trusted me. I made a promise to you." His Catholic guilt had resurfaced since they had gone all the way over a month ago. He thought that by going to confession and promising God that it would never happen again; by vowing to Jen it would never happen again, that it would all be better.

"This is both our faults, Tom. I could have stopped you, but I didn't."

He cried, wept for her, that he had taken something of Jen's that he had no right to take. He cried for the life they could have had, for the child who was conceived and not asked for.

"What are we going to do?" her small voice asked.

"I guess we'll have to get married." He blurted it out without realizing the tone of his voice.

"You make it sound like a death sentence."

"I'm sorry. It's just that I..."

"I don't think we should decide anything yet. The only thing that's certain is this baby, even though he was not planned, is a baby and I'm not going to have an..."

"*I wouldn't ask that, Jen. I know that abortion is wrong, so it's not even in the equation.*"

They held each other in the quiet of his apartment.

"*You know,*" she whispered, "*I always used to fantasize how I would tell you the first time I was pregnant after we were married. I never once thought it would happen like this.*"

"*I'm sorry. I hate the fact that we did this. I hate the fact that I couldn't control...*"

"*Stop,*" she said, then held her finger to his lips. "*We need to figure out the best thing for us to do. We need to get used to this first. Then we can decide later.*"

"*All right.*"

Leaning against the dryer, Tom began to drown in a sea of despair, unable to breathe. But as he sank, he prayed. *Jesus, Mary and Joseph, pray for us* was all he could muster at that moment. Immediately, hope rose up from within him. "God," he prayed, "Please tell Jen I love her and to keep strong. I love you, Jen..."

"Tom, come quickly!" His mother's voice was loud and piercing, calling him from the top of the stairs. He rushed up the steps taking two at a time. She met him at the doorway to the basement. "They're showing a video of Jen on CNN news!"

Tom followed his mother. Before he stepped into the living room, he could hear his wife's voice and his whole body tensed. His mother-in-law and the children were standing in front of the television.

When he finally saw the image, he drew in a breath. Transfixed, he watched as if he had never seen it before.

On the video clip, Jen said, "Oh, I love it, Sweetie. It's beautiful." Tom, who had been filming, had pulled in for a close shot. Jen was dressed in her pink and yellow flannel pajamas. "Open this, Mommy," said Callie – or maybe it was Cassie, he couldn't remember – the back of her head blocking Jen's face for the moment. "Okay, honey." Jen unwrapped the gift and her mouth widened in a huge smile. "It's just what I wanted! How did you know, Callie?" It was a simple bar of soap, but his wife acted like her daughter had given her the most incredible gift in the world. The camera zoomed in closer. The entire screen was taken up by her face. She was grinning from ear to ear, oblivious to the camera. Then Tom's own voice, "Hey, beautiful," he called, amidst the shouting. She turned and looked at the camera. She winked and blew a kiss, then mouthed "I love you." The commentator began to speak, but Tom couldn't listen. His mother clicked the television off.

Everyone remained silent. Tom was mesmerized. She was so vibrant and beautiful and....he had to stop himself from thinking of her in the past tense.

"I miss Mommy," said Chloe.

"Me too," Callie said, in a half-whisper.

Jen's mom was blotting her eyes. His mother cleared her throat. "I'd better pop that casserole in the oven."

Tom couldn't move. He wanted to watch it again and again. He looked down at his children's expectant faces. Leaning down, he gathered them into his arms in an embrace meant to console them. Instead, their small hands and bodies, these little persons, the combination of Jen and him, the representation of their love together, soothed him and his hope returned, renewed.

* * *

Jenny heard a car start and immediately sat upright.

Was Denise leaving? And if so, for how long? Jenny finally decided that it didn't matter. She must try to escape.

Searching the room with her eyes for something that might open up the lock on the chain, she leaned over to touch the chains on her ankles, but her stomach was too big and she wasn't able to reach it. She yanked on the chain with her feet to try to break it, but it was no use. Her ankles were swollen and there was no way she could slip them out.

Where would Denise keep the key?

* * *

Having already started up the car, Denise tossed the empty cigarette package out the window. It was blasted hot. Who would have thought it would be hot in September in Ontario?

There was rumbling in the distance. Thick black clouds hung low in the sky. Perhaps there would be some relief.

She was sweating now, and had started to shake. She needed to have a cigarette. With all the advanced planning, she had stocked up on formula, baby clothes, diapers and food. Denise couldn't believe that she had forgotten to buy enough cigarettes. Then again, she had been chain smoking since yesterday morning.

Cigarettes were easy enough to buy at the general store three kilometers up the road. She'd be back in ten, 15 minutes at the most. Besides, she needed to get out of that claustrophobic cottage. The smell was starting to cause her eyes to water.

Her mind tried to focus, but there were too many things swirling about in her head. She wished that she had paid more attention when Dr. Eastman was performing C-sections on the animals. And how much more different would it be to perform on a human? She had to admit that she was hoping she wouldn't have to do that. It would be much easier if the baby just came naturally.

Denise drove to the main road a short distance away. A crack of thunder roared, this time closer, and the rain now came down in sheets. She turned the windshield wipers to their fastest speed.

Twenty-Three

Jenny stood at the foot of the bed, her leg still shackled. Perhaps she could pull the cot into the other room and search for her purse, which contained her cell phone. And where would Denise keep the key to unlock the shackles on her legs? With any luck, if she found her cell phone, at the very least, she could call the police. She had no idea how far she was from home or even where she was, but perhaps the police could trace the call.

As she frantically pulled the small bed toward the door, she heard thunder in the distance, then the steady beating of rain on the roof. She stopped, lifting her head. The rain sounded like hands clapping, urging her on.

She dragged the cot the few feet to the door and winced. The chain on her ankle was biting into her skin.

At the bedroom door, she clenched her teeth and slowly turned the knob, hoping, praying. The door clicked open and swung inward. Jenny tried to pull the cot through the doorway and it jammed. She yanked on it. It wouldn't fit unless she turned it sideways. Jenny quickly pushed it back into the bedroom. It toppled and in her hurriedness, the bed rolled completely over. She hoisted it on its side again and dragged it through the doorway into a living room with a wood stove in the middle of it, a small kitchenette and an arm chair in front of a television. An army type cot was beside the chair.

Along the far wall were baby items, a car seat, diapers and cartons of baby formula. She cringed and forced herself to look away. *I need to find my purse.*

She scanned the room with her eyes and spied her purse beside the chair. She dragged the cot across the room, its scraping sounds hurting her ears. She crouched down and lifted up her purse. Her heart was beating wildly. *I'm going to get out of here. Thank God.* She just needed to find her phone. She reached inside, pushing her wallet, receipts and other papers aside, then finally dumped the entire contents on the floor. No cell phone. *Where is my cell phone?*

* * *

Kathy Romano stared at the computer screen and Denise Kramer's mug shot. A fax to the Sutherland Veterinary Hospital confirmed that this was indeed the woman who worked at the vet's office and who had apparently been pregnant. An internal records search confirmed that Denise was arrested for impaired driving in 2002. The photo was nearly ten years old, but she printed it to show Christine and Caleb Callahan, then called the Forensics Identification Unit to provide her with eleven other photos of similar looking women for the photo line up.

Later, at the Callahan household, Kathy separated Caleb and Christine, leaving the toddler in the living room watching television. She escorted the ten year old into the kitchen. Tom followed them and stood beside his daughter.

"Christine, I have some photos here and I want you to tell me if there is anyone in the photos that you recognize. And if you recognize someone, tell me where you recognize them from."

"Okay," the girl said, with an air of confidence in her voice. Kathy could tell that she wanted desperately to help find her mom, as if the whole world depended on her.

Kathy spread the 12 photos on the table.

Without hesitation, Christine pointed to the middle photo on the top line. "That's the lady I saw at the window of the house across from the bus stop a few days ago, and who followed us."

"Okay. Tom, would you get your son, please? Christine, you may return to the living room."

"Is that her? Is that the lady who took my mom?"

"We're not sure," Kathy responded.

Tom came into the kitchen, his son in his arms.

"Tom, would you take your daughter back to the living room?" He nodded, placed the boy down, and escorted his daughter out of the kitchen. Kathy waited for Tom to return before she showed the photos to the toddler.

Kathy leaned down and spoke softly. "Caleb, I have some photos here and if you see the woman who took your mommy, let me know which picture it is, okay?"

The little boy looked at his father, who smiled at him.

Kathy placed the 12 photos on the table, mixing the order. She repeated her instructions, although she wasn't sure the little boy would understand. "Caleb, I want you to look at these pictures and tell me if there is anybody you recognize. If you do recognize someone, where do you recognize them from?" Caleb stared at the photos, then immediately pointed to the far left photo on the bottom and said, "She took Mommy. She mean. Don't like her."

"Thanks, Caleb."

"Go back into the living room, Sport," Tom said. As the toddler rushed off, Tom glanced at Kathy like he wanted her to tell him it was all going to be all right. But she was only beginning to get an idea of what sort of woman they were dealing with.

Kathy knew that Tom needed some assurance, however, so she added, "I'm on my way to the Kramer house across the street from the bus stop where your wife was taken."

"Did they pick out the right photo?"

"They both pointed to Denise's picture."

"Thank you, Sergeant."

In the car, Kathy joined Bob Preston, who informed her that Denise Kramer owned a '99 Ford Taurus. Tread marks consistent with a Ford Taurus were observed where the cell phone was found.

* * *

As Denise steered along the winding road, she scoffed at the speed they expected her to go. She wasn't going to drive ridiculously slow when she needed to be back at the cottage immediately. She pressed her foot down on the accelerator. Her mind became a jumbled mess of medical terms: placenta previa, C-section, hemorrhaging. She couldn't think of that right now. The radio station was blaring a stupid Paul Anka song about some girl having his baby. She looked down as she adjusted the radio to the country station. When she glanced up again, smoke was coming out from under her hood. She groaned. She wanted to kick herself for forgetting to put the coolant in. How could she be such an idiot? But she refused to slow down. And it would only take a few minutes there and back, even in a rainstorm.

Her car hit a muddy pothole just as she was approaching a curve. Slickness on the road sent her speeding car skidding out of control and it was now flying through the air. Time passed like a slow motion movie. As the car slammed against a tree with a sickening crunch, windows smashed, sending shards of glass into the car. Denise was thrown forward, her face slamming into the dashboard, then she was whipped back against the seat before she finally lost consciousness.

* * *

Jenny's eyes began to tear, but she would not give in to despair. She pulled the cot to the front door, the metal legs scraping along the floor. Her stomach growled, her ankle throbbed, and she was beginning to feel dizzy. Jenny paused, waiting for a mild Braxton-Hicks contraction to pass, then said another prayer before opening the door. Surprisingly, it was unlocked. She found herself stepping onto a small porch and she cried with relief. She was going to escape, but she needed to hurry. She yelled, fear pitching her voice, no words, just a desperate call for help. Jenny slumped against the door jamb as the wind and rain seemed to smother her pleas. She screamed "Help" this time, as loudly as she could muster, but the only response was a fluttering of birds overhead. If she had to drag the cot down the road in the pouring rain, surely someone would see or hear her. She took a deep breath, inhaling the damp, earthy scent of rainfall. With a renewed sense of purpose, she grunted and yanked the bed through the doorway and onto the porch, but stopped when she felt wetness sliding down her legs. She stared downward. Blood stained her pants and began to trickle onto the porch below. "No!" Panic set in as she shoved the bed back inside. The door slammed closed and the cot landed beside the door.

What would she do now? She pulled her pants off, but with the chain still shackled to her ankle, she could only manage to remove one pant leg; the other now lay in a heap around her ankle. Jenny ripped the sheet from the bed and stuffed it between her legs. She sat down on the edge of the cot.

So far it was painless bleeding. She hadn't yet had a contraction, but the doctor had told her that if she started bleeding, especially now, that she must get to a hospital immediately because it meant that the placenta was beginning to detach.

She wanted to escape, but that wouldn't be possible now.

She cried out, her mouth open, her eyes widened. A mild contraction began ebbing its way downward. It peaked, then subsided and she caught her breath. She looked down at the sheet, now turning bright red. *Oh, God, please help me...*

Eleven years earlier

Tom and Jenny sat silently, heads down, in the car in front of her house. It was snowing, the large flakes coating the hood and windows around them.

In the coming weeks, they would make the difficult decision: would they get married, remain single but together and keep the baby, or give the baby up for adoption? After three weeks, no choice seemed a comfortable one. Every time they were together, it was as if they both reminded each other of the heart-wrenching decisions that lay ahead and they avoided talking about them.

"Tom?"

"Yes?"

"We need to talk about what to do."

"I know. But I have to go soon and I didn't want the last hour of our togetherness to be spent talking about..."

"Please."

"All right."

"I think we ought to..." Jenny paused.

"We ought to what?"

"I think we ought to get married. I know that it's not really the right time, but we know we eventually want to get married."

"Yes."

Jenny shifted in her seat as she felt mild cramping in her abdomen.

"You okay, Jen?"

"Yeah, I guess. I've never been pregnant before so I don't know what to expect. I feel like I'm getting my period."

"Is it possible that you are getting your period?"

"You mean one that is 12 weeks late? No."

The mild cramps were overtaken by painful waves now ripping through her lower abdomen.

"Jen?"

She winced then grabbed onto his shoulder, squeezing him, hoping perhaps it would lessen her pain.

"Yikes, Jen. What's going on?"

"I don't know. But it's hurting and I don't know if this is supposed to happen."

Just then, Jenny felt it, the gush of blood and within a few seconds, there was so much blood, Tom could now see it seeping through.

"You're bleeding!"

Jenny half-expected him to use his sweater to cover her, to fix this, to make it all better.

"I think we need to go to the hospital. But not the local hospital. Drive down to Fenton's Hospital an hour away or better yet, drive to Kingston where no one knows me."

"Are you crazy? I'm not taking you somewhere an hour away. You need to see a doctor right away. And someone has to tell your mom..."

"Don't tell her why you're taking me, okay? Just tell her we're going for a drive. She's going to be very upset, Tom."

"But she'd want to know, Jen."

"Please don't tell her, not yet."

"All right."

In the emergency room, a young female doctor approached the couple. Jenny immediately bonded to her. She was naturally pretty, with no make up and her brown hair pulled back into a pony tail. "My name is Dr. Leah Carter." Turning to Tom, she said, "I'm going to have to ask you to leave so I can examine her."

Jenny cringed. "Please don't make him go. I need him to stay with me."

"Fine," said the doctor, softening. "If you don't mind me asking personal questions with your..."

"He's my...boyfriend...fiancé." Using the word fiancé made the whole situation seem right. After all, she and Tom had already discussed marriage.

"...with your fiancé here, then I'll go ahead." She took the clipboard. "When was your last menstrual period?"

"Twelve weeks ago. September 2nd. I'm pregnant. I took three at-home pregnancy tests."

"I see. I'm going to have the ultrasound machine brought in so we can see what's going on." As the doctor stepped away, she pulled the curtain around the bed. Tom moved closer to her. Jenny lifted up the sheet and saw that *the bleeding seemed to have lessened, but the inside of her abdomen felt like it was exploding. She squeezed Tom's hand, her fingernails piercing the skin of his palm. "This hurts."*

"I know, Jen. I'm sorry you have to go through this."

At that, Jenny felt something hard come from within her. She lifted up the sheet and discovered the miniature baby unmoving and lifeless on the sheet. "Oh my God." They stared, silent, at the small form, shocked at the reality of the baby, their child, now dead in front of them.

They sat still and solemn. "Why do I not feel relieved, Tom? Why do I feel so much sadness?"

"I know. After all that, I can't believe..."

The nurse walked by and peeked her head inside the curtain. "Is everything all right?"

"I think Jenny just had a miscarriage."

The nurse returned in a few moments with a small basin and scooped the baby from the bed.

"Where are you taking it?"

"Hospital regulations require that anything expelled from a patient's body must be disposed of as medical waste."

Jenny began to sob. The nurse left. Tom pulled her to an embrace. They wept together for the child they would never know.

In the heat of the cottage, Jenny closed her eyes as another contraction gripped her body and more sticky wetness filled the bed. *This can't be happening.* Jenny had no idea how much time had passed, but she was alone and trying desperately to concentrate on what needed to be done for the impending birth.

She let out a piercing moan as the next contraction took over her body. She couldn't think of hemorrhaging right now, only of breathing and of getting through the contraction. As it eased, Jenny groaned, tears forming at the back of her throat, this time wondering when Denise was going to return and what would happen when she did.

Jenny willed herself to focus on the task at hand. Soon, another painful contraction came in a wave, peaked, then ended. How was she going to survive? How would her baby survive? *I can't do this, God. I can't...*

"I love you, Jen. Keep strong." Tom's voice was as clear as if he were standing there. With renewed strength, Jenny breathed deeply through the next contraction and allowed her body to take over and accomplish what it needed to. She couldn't concentrate on anything but breathing with each contraction. Each pain brought another gush of bright red fluid. Jenny was beginning to feel weak and dizzy. *God, help me* was all the prayer she could manage.

* * *

When Sergeant Romano left, Tom closed the door and allowed his eyes to glaze over as he stared ahead. He could hear the reporters shouting questions at her, but could not tell whether she had answered or ignored them. The phone rang and then he heard Jeff Anderson calling for him.

He rushed into the kitchen and picked up the phone. "Hello?"

"Mr. Callahan, my name is Frank Poston, a reporter for the *Ottawa Citizen* and..."

Tom gritted his teeth, and without saying a word, hung up. He looked at Jeff, who offered a sympathetic smile. They hadn't received a ransom call in the 28 hours since Jen had been abducted. He didn't know much about this sort of thing, but he guessed they wouldn't be receiving one. Jen was pregnant. This was a premeditated kidnapping, which could only mean one thing: whoever took her wanted the baby. Sergeant Romano skirted the issue the last time he asked, but he had watched enough crime shows on TV to know that the baby had to be the motivation.

With Jen not being able to have the baby naturally, she would die in childbirth if she wasn't found soon. If they didn't find her...no. Tom would not think of the ifs. They *would* find her.   His heart felt heavy, the huge crater of worry beginning to seep into every crevice, artery, muscle and bone in his body.

"Daddy?"

He looked down to see Christine's pained expression.

"Yes, honey?"

"They'll find Mom, won't they? They have to find her." Chris's lip was quivering, but she was trying to keep from crying. Tom crouched down and stared into her somber face. His oldest daughter's expressions reminded Tom so much of Jen.

Eleven years earlier

Tom hugged Jen tightly, held together by the new bond he wished they had never shared. As they wept for the child they had lost, Dr. Carter approached Jen's hospital bed.

"The nurse tells me you just had a miscarriage."

Jenny nodded and wiped her eyes with Tom's handkerchief. Tom knew that this was all his fault. He should have been more in control. Now, he had to step up to the plate and be a man. He needed to be Jen's voice in an atmosphere which didn't respect her rights not only as a patient, but as a mother. "She came and took our baby and told us it would be...disposed of."

"Jenny, Tom, when you have a miscarriage in the hospital, it's standard procedure to study the products of conception, then dispose of them."

"Dispose?"

"I'm sorry."

"Products of conception?" Tom asked. "It was a baby, a small tiny baby!"

"These are simply the medical terms we use."

"Your medical terms are wrong," Tom said, an edge to his voice.

Dr. Carter turned her attention to Jenny. "If you're

still bleeding, you may need to have a minor medical procedure, but I'm going to order that you be given more fluid by intravenous. Then we'll take a look at the uterus and see how it's doing," she said. "I'll return in a few moments.

Tom kissed the top of Jenny's head. *"I'm sorry, Jen. It's my fault that you had to go through this."*

"We did this together."

The doctor returned, squirted some liquid onto Jen's stomach, then rolled the wand over her abdomen.

Jenny moaned. *"I'm still having some cramps."*

"You may have some retained products of conception," she said in a matter-of-fact tone of voice. *"But we'll take a look here."*

The doctor remained silent for several long moments, her expression unreadable, almost neutral, as if she was studying a blank screen. *"I see from your chart that you're 19 and unmarried. Was this an unplanned pregnancy?"*

Jenny looked at Tom and her face reddened. He hated that the mere question had embarrassed her. Tom's shoulders straightened and he stood up.

"Yes, Ma'am...Doctor...it was, but..." He hesitated.

"But?"

"We wish we could have been given another chance. We wish..."

"I think that's what's happened here."

"I don't mean that. What I mean is that God gave us this gift, even though it wasn't planned. Then He took it away."

"Look," the doctor turned the screen so that both Tom and Jenny could see it.

"What it means," she said, pointing to the black bean shaped figure in the middle of the screen, *"is that you miscarried a twin. Here is the empty sac right here. But this fetus seems to be doing fine,"* she said.

Tom and Jenny sat wide-eyed as she pointed to their miniature child and the rapidly beating heart.

The doctor lifted the wand from Jenny's stomach, wiped the gel off, and tugged her hospital gown back over her.   Dr. Carter stepped away and pulled the curtain around the gurney.

Tom and Jenny embraced and wept together, this time with joy.   For a few moments, Tom couldn't think of anything except that he was now being given a second chance by God.   Now, it was clear. This baby, their child, was still alive, and hopefully would be born. Although their other precious baby was now in heaven, God had a special plan for this little one. He placed his hand on Jen's stomach, recalling the image of the rapidly beating heart.   Now, there was only one thing left to do.

"Jen?"

"Yes, Tom?"

"I don't care how difficult it will be."

"What?"

"Will you marry me?"

Tom lifted his daughter up and held her to his chest. Chris was too big for this, but he didn't care. She laid her head against his shoulder and finally began to sob.

"Shhh. It's going to be all right, honey."   Of all his children, it was Chris who made him realize that sometimes God gave gifts which weren't asked for. For many years, there was sadness in his heart that he and Jen didn't wait until marriage to physically express their love. But whenever he looked into the face of his oldest daughter, he was reminded that although he and Jen did something wrong, God chose, through them, to create an irreplaceable eternal human being. And he could never forget that.

Twenty-Four

Denise Kramer's house across from the bus stop was a nice enough semi-detached home. It had little in the way of feminine extras such as flowers in the garden or pastel type curtains in the windows. If Kathy didn't know better, she would guess this was a bachelor pad, not a woman's home. Kathy concluded that Mrs. Kramer was not a woman who liked the feminine frilly touches.

She knew the warrant would arrive any minute, but until then, she decided to investigate the outside of the house and interview any neighbors.

Kathy and Bob approached the porch. She knocked on the door and could hear a small yappy type dog barking its fool head off. *Sounds like an effective watch dog.*

"Doesn't look like anyone's home," Constable Preston observed.

The dog continued barking, but otherwise, there was no sound, no approaching footsteps. Kathy peered into the window and could see a small terrier mix.

Kathy banged more loudly this time. "Mrs. Kramer, this is the police. Are you in there?" As she yelled, a girl in her teens with long blonde hair was just coming out from the other half of the semi-detached house. She wore low cut jeans and a shirt which allowed for a generous portion of her abdomen to be exposed. Her belly button was studded with metal. Kathy said, "Excuse me, Miss?"

"Yeah?" the girl said, her eyebrows raised. It was then that Kathy noticed the girl had some metal jewelry attached to the right eyebrow as well.

"We're looking for Mrs. Kramer. Do you have any idea when she might be home?"

"I told the police guy who was here yesterday that I haven't seen her in a few days. Is this about the missing pregnant lady?"

Without waiting for a response, the girl continued. "Because the police officer questioned me yesterday. I told him I didn't see anything. I had just gotten home from school when I saw all the cars. But my mom's been watching the news constantly. I told her the police ought to be looking for a dead body by now."

Good thing you're not in charge here, Ms. Piercings.

"Could I ask you a few questions?"

"Sure, although I don't know much about Mrs. Kramer, except that she was pregnant. My mom will probably be better able to answer your questions. I'm sure she wants to help. Should I get her for you?"

"Yes, thank you." A few seconds passed, then Ms. Piercings brought her mom out to the porch. The older woman was actually normal looking, and shorter than her daughter by several inches. She was fairly fit for her age with a shoulder length stylish haircut and Sarah Palin type glasses.

"May I help you?"

"I'm Sergeant Kathy Romano with the OPP, she said, flashing her badge. "This is Constable Preston. What's your name, ma'am?"

"Loretta Pacella."

"I'm investigating the disappearance of Jenny Callahan, Mrs. Pacella."

"That's all over the news, even on CNN. I've been watching it non-stop, you know, while I'm making breakfast, lunch and dinner. We even had it on yesterday at the travel agency."

"Do you know your neighbor, Mrs. Denise Kramer?"

"Not anymore than to say hi or bye or how was your holiday. She's not the chatty sort. But she talks more than Mr. Kramer did. They've been separated about two years now, divorced for a year or so."

"What about Mrs. Kramer?"

"She was pregnant, I know that."

"Oh? How did you know?"

"As I said, she's not the chatty sort, but around four months ago, she was bouncy and happy and couldn't wait to tell me the news that she was pregnant, due in October."

"I see. Have you seen Mrs. Kramer recently?"

"I haven't seen her in the last two days or so. But I remember something odd..."

"Please go on."

"Well, two weekends ago, I watched her pack up her car with boxes and boxes of stuff. When I asked her if she was going on a vacation, she said, no, that she wasn't, that she was just stocking up the cottage. But the strange thing is she is pregnant and was lifting all these boxes into her car. I told her she ought to wait until my husband returned home and he would help her, but she ignored me."

"Were these boxes unmarked or did they..."

"You know, come to think of it, one box was a bulk box of those chocolate chip granola bars. My sister's got six kids and she buys those, too."

"Anything else?"

"She asked me if my sister had any of her kids at home, you know, a home birth. But, I said, no, that my sister had all her kids in the hospital, so she just shrugged and said thanks."

"What else do you know about Mrs. Kramer? Do they have any children?"

"No, they don't, which was why she was so excited to be pregnant. Last year, she seemed pretty depressed for the longest time about it. I told her a few times that if she wanted kids, she could have mine, but she declined." Loretta laughed, but Kathy didn't reciprocate.

"Mrs. Pacella, we need to get into her house and we're waiting on a warrant."

"We are her landlords so I have a key."

"Thank you, Mrs. Pacella."

"I can let you in, if you'd like."

A siren screeched as an OPP car rounded the corner.

"This must be our warrant." The car pulled to a stop and a female constable got out. Kathy met her halfway and grabbed the warrant without speaking. The female officer waited at the police car.

Loretta offered, "I hope you find that missing woman."

"Thank you."

It had begun to rain as Loretta opened the door, and Kathy and Bob Preston followed close behind her as they entered. The entranceway led into a small living room. Loretta drew in a breath as she surveyed the surroundings. Immediately, Kathy was struck by the smell of garbage, no doubt from the five black trash bags carelessly strewn at various spots in the living room. A tiny dog cowered under a chair near the window. Papers, clothing, boxes and other paraphernalia were piled on the sofa. Books, papers and dirty dishes were strewn haphazardly on the coffee table. Several opened pop cans and a few ashtrays dotted the table.

"Disgusting," Loretta blurted out.

"Mrs. Pacella, would you be so kind as to wait outside while we do our job?"

"Of course." The woman backed out, shaking her head. Kathy tried to breathe through her mouth. Although the garbage stench was bad, it wasn't as bad as decomposing dead bodies, so she tried to be thankful for small favors.

"This is something else, isn't it?" Bob said.

"Indeed."

"I don't see a television," the officer said.

"Perhaps she watches most of her television shows online."

"I don't see a computer."

"Maybe it's in the kitchen. Go take a look."

Having already taken a pair of disposable gloves out, she tugged them on, and crouched down. She moved aside some clothes and boxes to find a cable hook up and wires near the chair.

She picked up the Sutherland High School '99 yearbook from the coffee table and turned to a book-marked page. Circled was a graduation photo; below the picture, the name "Jenny Hathaway." Kathy's heart stopped. "Bob, look at this." He approached her as she held the book up. "Why would Denise have a copy of Jenny's yearbook? They weren't classmates, were they?" she asked.

"I don't know. Constable Anderson said that he went to school with both Mr. and Mrs. Callahan. Should we call the station and have them send a few more officers?"

"Yes, this could be considered a crime scene, if Mrs. Kramer is indeed the perpetrator, so have them send a small unit. I'll ask the constable who's waiting outside to remain here as well."

"I don't imagine that Mrs. Kramer has any hand sanitizers, eh?" Bob joked.

"Probably not, but there's some in the patrol car, which I intend to use."

Bob laughed.

She stepped toward the book case. "What to Expect When You're Expecting," "Baby's First Year," just about every book in this bookcase was either related to getting pregnant or having a baby or parenting. If Denise *was* expecting, these books would not be out of place.

"Sergeant?"

"Yes?"

"You might be interested in this." Constable Preston led Kathy into the kitchen. Amidst dirty dishes and boxes and papers, a computer sat on the table, an older style heavy, thick-screened monitor. It looked like some sort of gravy or sauce had spilled down the side of it. Kathy cringed, then sat down and she clicked on the Internet Explorer icon. She called up the history for the last week. There wasn't much of interest, except for the weather channel. She clicked on the day before yesterday. A few home birth sites, high school reunion sites.

She now had enough evidence to issue a warrant for the arrest of Denise Kramer.

"Pack it up in some plastic, Bob. We're taking the computer downtown to our IT specialist."

As Bob was placing the computer and monitor into the trunk, another patrol car drove up with additional officers to remain at the scene. Kathy sat in the patrol car and reviewed her notes. She focused on the conversation with Loretta. She had no doubt that Denise Kramer was the person who abducted Jenny Callahan and had taken her somewhere. For a case like this to be iron clad, however, she knew that she needed more hard evidence. And unfortunately, she had no idea where Denise had taken Jenny. She entered the information into the police car's computer. First she searched the database of property ownership records with the name Kramer. The search came up with over a thousand records. Perhaps a cell phone search to see if she could come up with some information to track down the former Mr. Kramer would be faster.

As well, she wanted to email a photo of Denise to every television and police station in North America as soon as possible.

*   *   *

Tapping of rain on the windshield woke Denise. She moaned and roused enough to open her eyes. "Where am I," she muttered. Her head felt like it was exploding and she could feel a trickle of wetness across her eyes. Lifting her head, she could see a huge oak in front of her and thick woods all around. Blood was smeared along the dashboard. Her chest felt like it was the Siamese twin of the steering wheel. She swore under her breath when she remembered that her car's seat belt was clasped and behind her, having had no chance to protect her. She thought she was going to be sick.

25 years ago

Denise leaned over the toilet bowl and threw up her entire breakfast. She tried to keep quiet, but just how was one supposed to keep quiet doing that? Last week, she had a positive pregnancy test at the Women's Health Clinic.

At first, she liked the idea of being pregnant, but didn't so much like the idea of throwing up. She told her boyfriend, but he started screaming at her when she said she wanted to have it. Then he gave her money and told her to "take care of it," or he'd leave her. Denise thought it was strange that he told her to "take care of it." She knew what he meant, but taking care of something usually meant protecting it. What else could she do? The receptionist at the Women's Clinic scheduled her for an abortion later that week.

The previous week one of the ladies with the rosary beads who stood on the sidewalk in front of the Women's Clinic tried to tell her that she could give it up for adoption. She thought about that, but her boyfriend made it clear what he wanted her to do.

Denise closed her eyes again and fell into a dreamy unconsciousness.

*   *   *

It was like an oven in the cottage, baking the stench and causing her to retch with every contraction. Jenny's body was now soaked with sweat, vomit and blood. Without a watch or clock, she had no idea how far apart the pains were. But she was still alive, despite the severity of the pains and the blood loss.

Jenny was frightened. And she felt weaker with each contraction, becoming too exhausted to cry out.

One minute she was sweating and the next, she was shivering so violently that her teeth were chattering.

It was nearly dark. Soon there would be no light in the room, no way to see her baby when... *Oh God, please let me get through this...or at least let my baby survive.   If you have to, take me, but please let my baby live...*

Twenty-Five

Greed has always been a motivator, Tom thought, as he hung up the phone and exhaled. Father Paul had received a donation from someone in the parish — one of the wealthier parishioners — to set up a $25,000 reward for any information which would lead to finding Jenny. As well, Tom's employer had already donated funds to the rescue effort.

Although he was grateful for the reward, it bothered him that perhaps someone might be prompted to come forward so they could get the money. But if it assisted the police in finding Jenny, at this point, he didn't care.

"Dad, gotta go pee."

"All right, Sport" he said. Despite the recent turmoil, Caleb continued to progress well with toilet training. His son wouldn't let his Grandmom or Nana take him to the bathroom, so it became a Dad activity. Tom shut the door and helped Caleb to pull his small pants down. He insisted on doing it the way his dad did, so the toddler stood on the stool in front of the toilet. He couldn't help but smile at how small his son looked. Then his mind thought of the baby inside Jenny, the seven or eight pound bundle that would be born soon. He exhaled, his heart heavy, then pulled up his son's pants. He helped him off the stool and lifted him up to wash his hands. "There you go, Caleb."

He opened the door amidst screaming from Christine. "Dad, come quick!"

"What, what?"

"The lady I told you about, her picture is on the news. That's the lady I saw, Daddy, look, look, that's her!"

Tom moved in front of the television set. Caleb yelled, "She take Mommy."

Tom didn't know whether he should feel relieved or more worried. If this woman was watching the news, she now knew that she was a suspect. Perhaps she might hurt Jenny and try to escape. *And, God forbid,* he thought, *perhaps she already has hurt her.* He wanted to tear her apart, he wanted to...

Suddenly, a voice rose up within him. *You've got to stop being angry and pessimistic. Hopeful. You must remain hopeful.*

* * *

At the OPP Command Center, an investigation of Denise's most recent Google searches on her computer revealed hundreds of searches for home birth and emergency birth. Most disturbing were the searches Denise did on Jenny and Tom. The 21st century stalker didn't have to leave the comfort of her home.

The OPP performed their own internet searches to find out information regarding the former Mr. Kramer. Unlike his wife, Mr. Kramer did not have a police record. But Kathy was able to track down his former employer, who gave her his cell number. She quickly dialed the number, then a message came on saying that the phone was not in a serviceable area. She gave instructions to another officer to call it constantly until they got an answer.

* * *

Jenny had drifted off, but woke to another excruciating contraction. The pains were getting longer and there was little time between them to think any rational thought except for *Please God, let this be okay. Let my baby live. Please, God.*

The mineral scent of blood filled the air. In the distance, she heard a baby crying. But there couldn't be a baby yet.

Darkness had now set in and she wasn't able to see.

Her lips were dry and she was so thirsty. She continued to shiver and yearned for a warm blanket. Another contraction welled up within her, and her body took over again as her entire stomach seemed to be pushing the baby out. Underneath her bottom was a thick, sticky puddle. Her ears were now ringing and she was becoming weaker with every painful contraction.

* * *

The kids again safely tucked into his and Jen's large bed, Tom had propped himself up with several pillows behind his back. He was afraid to sleep, as if Jen's safety depended on his staying awake and alert. Then again, he had no desire to sleep, not with his wife in harm's way. But he only had an hour or so the previous night and no chance or time to rest during the day. Despite his defiance, he found himself drifting off.

Tom was standing in a dark, narrow hospital hallway. At the end of the hallway was a hospital bed. The person on the bed moaned.

"Jen, oh, my God." I must help her. But as he tried to move, he found that his legs seemed nailed to the floor. "Jen, I want to help you, please, please God, let me help Jen."

"Tom, oh, Tom, please... help... me," Jen cried out.

Tom woke with a start. "Oh no, Jen. Could you be in labor?" He picked up the phone and dialed Sergeant Romano's cell. Her voice mail came on. "Damn it, yes, this is an emergency," he muttered as he pushed number one and was promptly disconnected. He tried again and was disconnected a second time.

Twenty-Six

Kathy took a sip of coffee and set it on the desk.   She had a feeling that they were on the brink of receiving a lead which would allow them to find Jenny.

Just after Denise's photo appeared on television, she spoke with Anne Kramer, Denise's cousin. The woman had taken the initiative and had called the OPP Detachment. Asked if she knew where Denise's cottage was, she replied that she didn't. However, she shared with Kathy that her cousin had asked her to look after the dog, and that she "didn't know how long she would be away."

"Sergeant Romano?" Bob Preston asked from across the room, holding a phone to his chest.

"Yes?"

"I think you'll want to interview this fellow in person."

"What fellow?"

"His name is Frank Heff. He claims to have seen Denise Kramer yesterday around 3:30 p.m."

After spending a few moments on the phone getting Mr. Heff to recount the story to Kathy, she motioned for Bob to accompany her to the police cruiser.

Half an hour later, they were at the home of Frank Heff, whom Kathy learned was a self-employed electrician.

"Mr. Heff, why don't you tell me again what you told me over the phone?"

The young man then recounted his story of stopping on a rural road a few kilometers from the Cedar Lake Exit on the Queensway, getting out to help a woman. Earlier today, he had seen Denise's photo on the news and asked to speak with the person in charge of the investigation.

"Mr. Heff, could you tell us exactly where it was that you saw her?"

"Yes. It's on my iPhone's GPS log. She was going in the

opposite direction, towards the Cedar Lake area. Here it is."

Kathy took down the information, then ordered all available units to the area.

With Bob Preston in the driver's seat of the police cruiser, Kathy dialed Tom Callahan's number. He answered on the first ring. "Tom, we have information that we hope will lead us to the cottage in which your wife is being held. We're on our way to the area now."

"Sergeant, I've been trying to call you. I just had a dream that Jen's in labor. You've got to get to her or... she could die. Please..." His voice cracked. "Please, help her."

"What do you mean you had a dream?"

"I had a dream that I was in a hospital somewhere. Jen was in labor. I couldn't do anything to help her. Please, Sergeant, you've got to..."

"Tom, that doesn't necessarily mean she's in labor."

"I know, but I have this horrible feeling that she is. Please find her."

"I'll contact you the minute we do." If Bob drove fast enough, they might be able to make it to the area within 15 minutes.

* * *

Denise finally accomplished the difficult task of opening her eyes. She swore under her breath. It was pitch black and her head hurt like hell. She felt wetness all over her face and it stung. All of a sudden, it felt like the TV dinner, granola bars and chips were going to come back up. But she concentrated and tried to breathe calmly. As she tried to take a deep breath, Denise couldn't seem to inhale. Finally, she was able to take a small breath and savored it like a fine chocolate. Faint sirens in the distance burned into her consciousness. Her eyes widened.

Twenty-Seven

Jenny roused as another contraction made its way from the top of her stomach downward. She opened her mouth to cry, but in her weakened condition no sound came out. *God, help me.*

Another excruciating pain took control of her body. It felt like someone was ripping the baby from her. Now an overwhelming urge to push took over. Nothing else mattered. Whether the baby was ready to come or not, whether she was able to give birth or not, she needed to push. *Push, breathe, push*, were her only coherent thoughts. Pushing this baby free from her body became the only goal that mattered now.

* * *

Denise tried to turn her head back and forth to escape the bright light. She squinted as a voice yelled at her through the window. "Ma'am, are you hurt?"

Did that fool have to yell? Her head throbbed and she was finding it hard to breathe.

She managed to nod. Denise tried to say something but all she could say was "hurt."

"We'll have you out of there in a second...what is your name?" In response to him, a moment of rationality hit her. She couldn't give her real name. She must give the name on the fake I.D's.

"Jo...anne Cox," she managed to say.

"All right, Joanne. The front of your vehicle is heavily damaged so it's gonna take a minute to get you free and into the ambulance." A moment later, someone was trying to put some sort of cuff around her arm. "BP's 80 over 60, pulse..." she heard. She remembered that she didn't bring her driver's license. And the glove compartment containing the registration looked wrecked beyond recognition. Her true identity was safe, at least for the moment.

* * *

In the darkness of the cabin, Jenny bore down with every ounce of strength she could muster. She felt weak and her teeth were chattering. However, she had no choice. She must push. *God, please help me...*

She took a deep breath, pushed again, and with momentary rationality, realized that once the baby was born, she would need something to tie off the umbilical cord. If the placenta broke away from her uterus before she cut the cord, the baby would die from lack of oxygen. She couldn't search for one now; her leg remained shackled to the bed. Did she hear sirens in the distance?

Jenny concentrated with all remaining traces of effort and pushed her baby out. *Thank you, God, for allowing my baby to be...* It was her last thought before slipping into unconsciousness.

* * *

Kathy and Bob drove on one of the rural road towards Cedar Lake. As they approached the scene of an accident, Bob took his foot off the accelerator.

"There are three cruisers and a paramedic there. Keep going, Bob. Jenny needs us more than they do."

Up ahead, Kathy could already see lights flashing and many police cruisers, gathering for the search. The rain had stopped, but Kathy knew the officers would have to proceed with caution as the dirt roads would be full of mud and water.

Denise had told Frank Heff that she lived five kilometers toward Cedar Lake, so she ordered the cruisers to travel three to four kilometers up the road, then begin searching side roads and marking the roads they had already searched with crime scene tape. She reminded them to keep constant radio contact with her.

They remained on the main rural road, driving slowly and listening to the police radio for any signs that Jenny had been found. "Nothing," "No houses," "Nothing," then

"Sergeant?" one officer from the Detachment radioed in.

"Yes?" she answered.

"We finally got a hold of Mr. Kramer. He said that the address to the cabin is 64 Farewell Lane."

"Great." She punched in the address in the GPS and immediately radioed the other officers to meet her there. *Farewell Lane.* Kathy hoped it wasn't a bad sign of things to come.

She immediately phoned the paramedics and instructed them to 64 Farewell Lane "ASAP."

They turned onto Farewell Lane and tried to read the numbers. "42, 44...Keep going, Bob. It'll be on the right side."

Constable Preston stepped on the accelerator. This part of Farewell Lane was a dirt road, now thick and wet and muddy.

Bob said, "There's 62. It can't be far."

"Step on it, Bob."

Several cruisers were now following them on the narrow road. They drove for what seemed like an extraordinarily long time, and when she saw the 64 on the right side, she almost yelled "Yes!" Driving forward, Kathy thought that they might get stuck in the mud, but Constable Preston floored the accelerator and managed to climb the hill and park in front of the cabin.

A police car pulled in behind them. The two officers approached her and Bob Preston.

Kathy turned to Bob. "Call the paramedics again and make sure they're on their way."

She made her way up to the porch, her shoes sinking into the mud. Pulling them up, she rushed up the steps. The cabin seemed dark, ominous and foreboding. Kathy drew her weapon and started up the small porch with Bob now behind her. She yelled out as her foot fell through a hole in one of the steps. Bob caught her as she began to fall.

"You all right?" Bob asked.

"Fine." She banged on the door. "Mrs. Kramer, this is the Ontario Provincial Police. We have a warrant to search the premises." Hearing no response, she turned the unlocked door knob, but something prevented her from opening it further. It looked like the metal bars of an army type cot.

Bob reached in and pushed the bed to allow the door to open. Kathy flicked on the lights and gasped at the scene. The copper scent of blood, vomit and urine wafted over Kathy like a sour breeze as she knelt beside the small cot where Jenny lay, still and unmoving, her baby lying in a pool of blood, looking gray and motionless between Jenny's legs, and still attached by the umbilical cord. Kathy's heart sank. She heard, "Clear," as the officers searched the small cabin and ascertained the perpetrator was not there.

Kathy slipped her gun back inside her belt, then crouched down again beside the young woman. Kathy wasn't a praying woman, but her first thoughts were, *Please God, don't let her be dead.* Her eyes focused on the chain on Jenny's leg. "Bob, I've got a pair of bolt cutters in my trunk. Get it quickly!"

Two ambulances screeched to a halt in front of the cabin, their sirens abruptly stopping. Kathy leaned her head out the door and yelled to two male paramedics to come and take control of the infant. One immediately cut the cord and began to work on the baby, who remained lifeless on the bed. The paramedic aspirated the baby's mouth, then the nose. Brisk rubbing of the back finally brought a quiet whimper from the infant. They bundled and whisked the baby away.

At the same time, Bob began to cut through the chain while a female paramedic worked frantically on Jenny, who lay unresponsive on the bed. Underneath her, a widening circle of red lay on the sheets and floor. She took Jenny's blood pressure, then shouted, "BP's 50 over nothing! Start an IV stat!" A male paramedic inserted an intravenous catheter into Jenny's arm while Bob attempted to slice through the thick chain around Jenny's ankle. He finally snapped through the metal and stepped away.

The female paramedic checked Jenny's blood pressure again. "I can't get a BP! Pupils are fixed and dilated! Transport her to the hospital now!" Kathy followed them out as they lifted her onto the stretcher and into the ambulance, its lights flashing and siren blaring. Kathy shouted, "Which hospital are you taking her to?"

"Queen Victoria," she shouted back.

Where was Denise Kramer? Perhaps she had heard the sirens and escaped into the woods surrounding the cabin immediately before they arrived. Kathy quickly handed out photographs to several police officers and ordered them to explore the surrounding area.

"Bob, remain here and secure the scene. I'll follow the ambulance to the hospital. Make sure this is cordoned off as a crime scene, and keep at least five officers here to wait for the Forensic Identification Unit."

Kathy quickly slid behind the wheel of the police car, and drove behind the screaming ambulance containing Jenny and her new baby, the sirens of the police car at full light and sound. She hoped the baby would be okay despite the difficult birth. It would be some consolation to Tom if his wife didn't survive the ordeal. In the short time that she had come to know him, it was evident that Tom loved his wife very deeply. *Let her live.*

She followed the ambulance to the nearest hospital, the Queen Victoria Hospital, on the outskirts of Ottawa.

With the police radio, she contacted the local OPP Detachment to send officers to the hospital.

Then she called Tom. She took a deep breath and attempted to calm herself. No matter how long she had been a police officer, these were always difficult calls to make. Kathy couldn't tell him that his wife would be okay, or even if she was still alive. She couldn't even tell him if his baby would make it. She needed to sound as positive as she could.

He answered on the first ring.

"Tom, we found Jenny." She could hear him draw in a breath, but he said nothing for a few seconds.

"Is she all right?"

Kathy didn't want to hesitate but nothing could come out.

"Sergeant?"

"Yes, Tom, I'm here. Jenny's been taken to the Queen Victoria Hospital. She's...lost a lot of blood."

"Oh, no. God, please..."

"But the baby's been born."

"I'll be there as soon as I possibly can."

Kathy turned the OnStar off and cringed. She hadn't asked the paramedics whether it was a boy or girl.

She followed the paramedics into the emergency ward and waited. Ten minutes after they had arrived, a young woman approached her.

"Sergeant?"

"Yes," she responded, looking up into the eyes of a young female physician.

"You're the officer in charge of the investigation into the Callahan abduction?"

"Yes."

"I'm Dr. Benson, the pediatrician in charge of the Callahan baby."

"Yes?"

"The baby's lethargic. However, she is stable and doing well, considering the birth."

"The father will be here momentarily."

"I'm sure he'll want to meet his daughter. Bring him up to the special care nursery when he arrives."

"Yes, all right."

Another daughter for the Callahans. Let this little girl know her mother.

Kathy returned to the entrance and waited.

Twenty minutes later, Tom and Constable Anderson

burst through the doors of the emergency room. Tom's eyes were bloodshot and watery, his red hair looked as if it hadn't been combed in days, his clothes hastily put on. One lone female reporter had managed to make it inside the hospital and had shoved a microphone in his face.

"Mr. Callahan, do you have any..."

For a brief second, from the angry expression on his face, Kathy thought that Tom was going to swing a punch at the woman. Constable Anderson stepped forward. "Leave Mr. Callahan alone." The officer took Tom by the arm and accompanied him across the room.

When Tom saw Kathy, his facial expression transformed immediately to one of relief. "Sergeant!"

"Tom."

"Any word on Jenny yet?"

"She's still in surgery."

Jenny Callahan's husband looked as if he was trying to remain composed, but his eyes were quickly filling with tears. Constable Anderson spoke up. "Sergeant, I'll stand by the doors to prevent other reporters from getting in."

"That's fine, Constable." Jeff made his way to the emergency room entrance just in time for it to swing open. Tom and Kathy turned to watch as the paramedics rushed forward with an injured person on a stretcher. Kathy overheard the paramedic speaking to the nurse. "Woman's name is Joanne Cox, her BP is 90/60, pulse 110. Car accident."

"Sergeant?" Tom asked.

"Yes?"

"Do you think Jenny is going to make it?"

Kathy hesitated as she wasn't sure how to respond. Tom's head was lowered and staring downward. At her pants. His face became pale. She sighed. *Damn, my blood-spattered pants.* "Tom?" He didn't respond, instead he continued looking at her shoes as if they were some sort of connection to his wife. "Tom?"

"Is that from...Jen?" He pointed to the blood on her pants.

"Tom, listen to me. The doctors are doing everything they can."

He nodded, his expression blank.

Kathy stepped close to him, putting her hands on his shoulders. "Tom, look at me." When he focused on her, she said, "You have another daughter."

"A daughter?"

"Yes, the baby's going to be fine. She's stable. She's in the special care nursery upstairs. Come. I'll take you there."

"Perhaps I ought to stay here to talk to the doctor. I want to see my wife."

"We'll tell the nursing staff at the desk that we're taking a quick trip to see the baby."

He nodded, allowing her to take charge. She spoke quietly to one of the nurses, then they took the elevator two floors up.

A few times, Kathy had to guide Tom by gently taking his arm and leading him on. They stopped at the nursery window. She left Tom at the doorway and told the nurse inside that Tom was the father of the Callahan baby. The nurse came forward and attached a hospital bracelet on his arm to identify him as the baby's father.

Kathy motioned for him to come forward.

* * *

Tom moved, but his brain remained numb. No one had told him how Jenny was doing. That couldn't be good. The nurse picked up the baby and held her out for Tom. He raised his hand and shook his head. Right now, he couldn't be sure he wouldn't drop her. Despite the numbness he felt, he gazed down into her small round face. Little Buddy's eyes were trying to open. He managed a slight smile. Little Buddy would need a proper girl name now. She looked like Chris as a baby. He found himself smiling. He blinked the tears away. He was grateful Little Buddy was going to be fine, but he was filled with anxiety at not knowing how his wife was doing. He bit down on his lip to stop himself from losing it.

"Tom, I've just received word that the surgeon would like to speak with you on the first floor." Sergeant Romano was leaning her head through the doorway of the maternity ward.

His stomach felt like it had a lead weight inside of it, pulling his hope deeper and deeper into darkness.

Soon, he could feel Sergeant Romano holding his elbow and urging him forward. He knew that he was walking, but couldn't somehow feel his legs moving. Finally, they stepped into the elevator.

This had to be a horrible nightmare. The doors of the elevator swung open. Tom stepped out of the elevator, Sergeant Romano behind him. A young Asian man in scrubs greeted them, offering his hand. He was small in stature, shorter than Jen. As he held out his hand, Tom attempted to read the expression on his face.

"Mr. Callahan, my name is Dr. Wong. I have just finished surgery on your wife." The doctor hesitated, his expression unreadable, and Tom felt like he was going to be sick.

"God, no, please don't tell me that Jenny is..."

"No, no, Mr. Callahan. Your wife made it through the surgery, but it was necessary for me to perform a hysterectomy."

"Oh." For a second, he sighed with relief. Jen was alive.

But with relief came sadness. His wife would be heartbroken.

"She has lost a lot of blood. I do not understand how she survived the birth and the drive to the hospital. She had no detectable blood pressure in the ambulance. There is no reasonable explanation for why she is alive right now. She obviously has a tremendous will to live."

"Yes, she does."

"The bleeding would not stop so the hysterectomy was

necessary to save her life. She has also been given seven units of blood. She is in recovery right now and should be awake shortly, if you would like to see her. I will take you there."

Tom was now doing his best to take it all in. He was relieved that his wife had made it through the surgery. "Yes, I would like that very much."

"And Mr. Callahan?"

"Yes?"

"Your wife is going to be weak for many months. She has lost a lot of blood. She will need to take it easy. How many other children do you have?"

"Five."

"Make certain she takes it easy."

"Of course, Doctor. She will. I promise you that."

"Come," he said, "I will take you to the recovery room.

* * *

As they walked to the recovery room, Kathy asked Dr. Wong if it would be too soon to question Jenny. He indicated that Jenny would need some rest, but that it would be fine to interview her in the morning. Kathy made a mental note to ensure that a police constable was stationed not only outside the recovery room, but also when she was moved to her regular room.

Twenty-Eight

Denise sipped water holding the cup with her right hand as the nurse took her blood pressure. She was craving a cigarette. The left side of her face had been banged up in the accident and the long cut near her hairline necessitated a large bandage which covered her entire forehead. When Denise looked into the mirror a few minutes ago, even she didn't recognize herself. She tried to hide a smile a few hours ago when the doctor in the emergency room was treating her. He looked into her eyes and checked her blood pressure at the same time the news flashed her photo on the television set outside the treatment room.

Denise Kramer was dead. Joanne Cox would survive.

A tall, good looking young doctor approached her bed.

"You were very fortunate, Ms. Cox," the doctor said. "You've got quite a laceration on your forehead, you've suffered a mild concussion, and the left side of your face is injured. I've ordered a pulmonary test to see if you have some damage to your right lung. And you've got three broken ribs. Otherwise, you seem to be doing fine."

"What about this bump on my leg?"

The doctor picked up the sheet and examined the black and blue mark on her left leg. "It's a hematoma, otherwise known as a bruise. You'll be fine."

Several people clambered past the room.

"Where are they heading in such a rush?"

"Press conference in 10 minutes for that missing pregnant woman."

Denise found herself smiling again. She had already listened to the news and knew that the baby had been born, and was currently in this hospital. However, the news channels were not revealing the sex of the baby. They also had not disclosed whether Jenny had survived, but that wasn't important.

Denise put the glass down and lay her head back against the pillow on the stretcher. Perhaps her one and only chance at motherhood wasn't gone. It was time to put Baby Plan B into action.

* * *

Jenny felt someone patting her right hand.

"Mrs. Callahan? Jenny?" a female voice asked.

Let me sleep she wanted to tell the voice. Then it hit her: pain, a sharp throbbing in the abdomen. She managed to open her eyes and tried to mouth the word "pain." She heard, "You'll feel better in a minute, Sweety. You're very lucky to be alive."

Alive. She was alive. But where was her baby?

She tried to mouth the word "baby" but it sounded like "bay."

Someone gingerly took hold of her left hand. She slowly turned her head but her heavy eyelids remained closed.

"Jen." It was Tom's warm voice. "I was so worried about you."

She nodded. She wanted to tell him how much she loved him and how thankful she was to be alive. But all she could mutter was "love."

"I love you too, Jen. I don't know what I would've done if...." He squeezed her hand. She could feel his lips kissing her ring finger, then her middle, index finger and thumb. Finally his warmth, his smell, his lips on her forehead. A sigh. Then silence, with only the beeping of the monitors, the blood pressure cuff squeezing, then letting go. Jenny couldn't tell how much time had elapsed. Moments? Or perhaps an hour? It felt like her gurney was floating. Finally, she opened her eyes. Tom was smiling at her, with those gorgeous hazel eyes blinking back tears.

"Hey."

"Hey."

"Are you ready to meet our newest daughter?"

"Daugh...ter?"

"Little Buddy is a girl. She looks like Chris."

"Doing okay?"

"She's sleeping a lot, but doing okay."

"Want to see her."

"I'll ask the nurses if they'll bring her to you."

Silence followed for three or four minutes, then Jenny whispered, "Pain, Tom. Why pain?"

She opened her eyes just as Tom glanced away. Then he made eye contact with her. "Jen..."

She closed her eyes, then opened them again.

"The doctor had to..."

"Had to?"

"The doctor couldn't stop the bleeding. He had to perform a..."   He stopped, lowered his head, then continued, "...hysterectomy."

She drew a breath in sharply and closed her eyes. Hysterectomy was such long, abrasive word. Jenny had so embraced her fertility and what it meant to be life-giving that it never dawned on her that she might lose that gift while she was so young. Her eyes remained closed, now beginning to tear. She could feel Tom's lips on her eyes, kissing her tears. "Love you," she whispered.

"Love you too."

"I'm...alive." She opened her eyes and peered into her husband's eyes and tried to smile.

"Thank God you're alive. I was so mean to you the morning you were kidnapped and I could've lost you. I'm so, so sorry."

"Already...forgotten...and forgiven."

"Oh, Jen, I love you so much." He kissed her lips.

Twenty-Nine

September 11th

While Jen slept, Tom held the baby in a large rocker brought from the nursery. He was grateful that the hospital staff had allowed him to remain with his wife throughout the night. Although he was exhausted, he only managed to nod off occasionally. Frequently, Jen woke up gasping, calling his name.

Flower arrangements began arriving first thing this morning. Tom surmised that most of these were from well-wishers. Except for the roses. Last night, he had asked his mother to order a dozen and have them delivered.

Tom looked at the time: 8:45 a.m., the approximate time the plane hit the first World Trade Center Tower on this date many years ago. At the time, Chris was a newborn, and he and Jen had watched the news coverage together from the moment he came home from school that day. He said a prayer of thanksgiving that the police had found Jen, then said a quick prayer for the souls who died that day many years ago.

There was a knock at the closed door. Sergeant Romano stepped inside.

Tom stood up, the baby still in his arms, and welcomed her. "Hello, Sergeant." Thankfully, she had changed her pants and was now wearing dark pants which were free of Jen's blood.

"Hello." She looked around at the copious flower arrangements. "Looks like a florist's place in here. Nice."

She leaned down and gazed at the baby, whose eyes were open and looking around. "She's a beauty."

The quiet chatter caused Jen to waken. "Tom?"

"I'm right here, Hon." He and Sergeant Romano walked to his wife's bed side.

The officer smiled as she glanced at Jenny.

"Jen, this is the person who helped find you. Her name is Sergeant Kathy Romano."

"Nice to meet you."

"It's a pleasure to finally meet you, Mrs. Callahan."

"Jenny."

"Jenny."

"What does Kathy stand for?"

"Katherine. Why?"

"I like it, for our baby."

"It's a great name, Jen," Tom said. "But you mean Cathy with a C? Certainly you don't intend to break the tradition of C names, do you?"

Jenny smiled.

"I've never had a baby named after me," Kathy smiled. "But if you'd like to do that, I'd be honored."

"Thank you for saving my life."

"It wasn't just me. I had a whole team working with me." Sergeant Romano hesitated. "Do you feel up to any questions?"

"Perhaps you should wait until later," Tom suggested.

"It's fine, Tom," Jenny said, her voice a whisper.

"Had you ever seen the woman who kidnapped you before?"

"Vet's office. Her name is Denise."

"She actually lives across from the bus stop. She's been stalking you."

"Stalking me?"

"For your baby."

Jenny's eyes widened, and her breathing quickened.

Sergeant Romano patted Jenny's hand. "That'll be all for now. I'll return later this afternoon. Perhaps you might feel up to answering more questions then?"

She nodded.

The sergeant started towards the door. "Wait," Jenny said.

"Yes?" Sergeant Romano returned to her bedside.

"Did you find her?"

"No, but we've issued a continent-wide alert for her. Her photo has been emailed to every television station and police station in North America. She won't get far. Don't worry. Until she is apprehended, you'll have an OPP officer guarding your door. He'll keep the press away too."

Jenny smiled. "Thank you."

Sergeant Romano left the room. Tom pulled the chair closer to her bed. "I'm staying with you. I'll sit right here by your bed."

"I'd like that." Her words came out slurred, like she sounded when she had a couple of glasses of sweet red wine.

"Your mom is with the kids. They'll be visiting later." Tom held onto her hand. He watched his wife drift off to sleep.

Thank you, God, for giving me back my wife.

Thirty

Lucky. I'm just plain lucky, Denise thought, as the nurse took her blood pressure again. "Are you having any trouble breathing, Ms. Cox?"

"Not too bad."

If she hadn't been in that accident, she might have returned to the cabin right around the time the police had arrived. Except for the fact that she was injured, her plan hadn't failed. It just changed.

The nurse checked the sutures on her forehead, studied the now bruised and swollen left side of Denise's face, then took her pulse. "The doctor has ordered that your IV be removed if you're drinking and eating regularly. So perhaps we can get that out of you this afternoon."

Denise forced a smile. A game show was blaring on the television of the elderly patient in the bed next to hers. The woman never changed channels and Denise surmised she must be sleeping most of the time.

"Ms. Cox, one of the hospital administrators will be visiting you shortly. The hospital needs you to supply them with your health card number. We did an OHIP database search and came up with thousands of people with the name Joanne Cox and hundreds around your age."

"I'll call my cousin to bring in my card," she said, knowing that she wouldn't be staying long enough.

* * *

Late that afternoon, Sergeant Romano returned to interview Jenny, asking her questions and writing them down in her notebook. Jenny was distracted. Her abdomen was quite painful and the drugs were clouding her mind.

"So when you heard the car start up, what did you do?"

"What?" Jenny asked.

"What did you do when you heard Denise's car start up?"

"I tried to think of a way to escape." As she recounted her attempt to pull the cot into the cabin's living room, Jenny's body tensed and her heart began to pound. All of a sudden, she was again yanking on the cot, pulling it toward the door. *I can't find my cell phone...where is my cell phone...don't look at the baby items...the rain on the roof...the relief at opening the door...the dread, utter fear at beginning to bleed.* She made a whimpering sound, and began to weep.

Her husband sat down beside her on the edge of the bed. "Hey, it's okay. You're safe here." Tom was rubbing her arm and she leaned her head against his chest.

"That'll be all for now, Jenny. I'll let you rest," Sergeant Romano said.

Jenny nodded. Tom accompanied the officer to the door; they spoke for a few minutes before he returned to her bedside.

The baby began to stir in the bassinet. Tom leaned over and spoke to the baby. "Hey, Little Lady, are you ready for a nursing?" She responded by squinting, then opening her small mouth. "She is not only beautiful, but smart, just like all my Callahan girls." He picked her up and cradled her in his arms.

Despite her painful abdomen, Jenny's heart was bursting with relief and gratitude.

"How about I help you nurse this gal before I go home and check on the kids?"

She nodded.

"Then the two of you can have a nice nap."

Tom held the baby close to his wife's breast and his daughter latched on like she had taken a course in Breastfeeding 101 while still in the womb. Baby Cathy nursed first on one side, then on the next. Tom took the baby, burped her and placed her in the bassinet. Tom kissed the top of his wife's head. "Love you."

"You too."

The door closed as her husband left. Jenny was just drifting off to sleep when a nurse whispered, "Sorry, Mrs. Callahan, but I need to check your incision." Jenny felt the woman lift up her gown and winced as she removed the bandage.

When the nurse left the room, Jenny thought again about Denise and her whole body tensed. She had to keep reminding herself that she was safe in the hospital, with an officer posted at the doorway.

There was a knock and Father Paul's smiling face greeted her. "Hello, Jenny!"

"Father Paul, it's good to see you."

"It's especially great to see you, Jenny. We were all worried about you. Many people were praying for you."

"I know. Thank you for your prayers."

He gazed down into the bassinet. "Looks like you have another beautiful Callahan baby...but this one doesn't have red hair."

"Not yet anyway."

The priest leaned down and blessed baby Cathy's small forehead. One of the things Jenny loved about Father Paul was that he was so comfortable around children and babies, the natural result of being the oldest of nine siblings.

The baby had opened her eyes and was now staring at the young priest. "Aren't you a pretty little girl?" he said, his voice high-pitched. The baby's eyes widened. "See? She's enamored with her parish priest already," Father Paul said with a grin.

"I see that."

Fr. Paul anointed Jenny and gave her Communion. Then he walked toward the doorway. "I'll let you to rest."

"I need to talk, if you have the time."

"Of course."

"I'm so grateful to be alive and that my baby is going to be all right, but..."

She glanced toward her daughter's bassinet.

"But?"

"I'm afraid. I can't breathe when I start to think about it. The woman who abducted me said she planned to kill me. My children would've been left without a mother. Tom would have..." She paused.

"Jenny, it's natural for you to be afraid. And you have every right to be angry."

"I know that I'm going to need to forgive her, but..."

"But what?"

"Sometimes I have a hard time forgiving Tom and I love him. How am I going to forgive her?"

"It'll take time, Jenny. Pray for the grace to do so." He paused. "Can I suggest something?"

"Of course."

"Pray for your kidnapper, pray for her soul."

Jenny scowled. "Pray for *her*?"

"Praying for the person who has hurt you can help to bring about forgiveness. Jesus forgave the men who crucified Him, who pounded the nails in His hands and feet, when He said, *Father, forgive them for they know not what they do.*"

"I don't know if I can do that, not yet, Father Paul."

"That's understandable. However, I can attest to the fact that it does work in bringing about forgiveness."

They chatted for a few more minutes, then he gave her and the baby a blessing and left.

In the solitude of the private room, she thought about Denise. Why hadn't she returned to the cabin? Had she seen the police cars and escaped? Just the thought of her captor being out there made Jenny's heart pound. She recalled Fr. Paul's suggestion to pray for Denise. It would be easy to pray that the woman would be found and put in jail, but to actually pray for her?

In many ways, Jenny understood Denise's obsession which came from an attitude that babies are a commodity, certainly not from a selfless wish to nurture and love a child. Her warped obsession had nearly cost Jenny and her baby their lives. The more she thought about the situation, the angrier she became. She couldn't imagine ever feeling any kind of forgiveness.

Forgive us our trespasses as we forgive those who trespass against us. The words of the Lord's Prayer echoed in her mind. *At least that's a start.*

All of a sudden, the flowers in her hospital room filled her senses. A vase of red roses, her favorite, a gift from Tom, adorned her bedside table. Bright and colorful carnations, roses and lilies covered every surface. She breathed in deeply of the fragrance, and found herself drifting off to sleep.

Sometime later, Jenny heard quiet footsteps and opened her eyes.

Tom kissed the top of her head.

She opened her eyes and smiled. "When will the kids be visiting?"

"I'll go back home around dinnertime to get them. Your mom wants to spend time with you too."

"Good. I've really missed them. Mom too."

He reached into the bassinet and picked up the baby, who had woken up and was looking around.

Tom helped her to latch on the baby.

"Thanks, Tom." She gazed down into the face of her newborn. "We make beautiful babies together, don't we?"

"We sure do."

Jenny's smile faded. "I just hate thinking that she will be our last."

"Me too."

*   *   *

A hospital worker returned to Denise's room with a tray of Jello and soup.

Denise savored the soup and Jello, then downed the apple juice. She was one of those people who actually liked hospital food, but she wasn't planning on staying long enough to try the real food.

The nurse came into her room. "How are you doing with your lunch?"

"Okay. I finished it."

"Great. I'll return after lunch to take out your IV."

Sitting on the edge of the bed, Denise swung her feet back and forth. The TV was still blaring, this time Wheel of Fortune was on, and a balding middle-aged man was asking if he could buy a vowel.

The pleasant smells of hot lunches made her mouth water. She glanced at the time, just before noon. The distraction of meal time would be just what she needed for Plan B to be successful.

She ripped off the surgical tape, pressed down and pulled the IV tubing out. She had done this a million times with animals. All she needed now was to apply pressure to make the IV site stop bleeding. If the nurse happened to come back before she left, she would tell her that it slipped out. Not surprisingly, ten more minutes passed and the nurse hadn't returned.

* * *

Tom dozed off in the chair beside his wife's bed. Jen had fallen asleep again and Tom was not far behind. After two sleepless nights, it didn't take much for him to nod off. Her soft breathing always relaxed him and made him drowsy.

Jenny was finally breathing deeply. The pain medication in the IV was doing its job.

His wife moaned in her sleep and she opened her eyes like it was some delayed reaction to a noise down the hallway. But her frightened expression revealed that she had had another nightmare. He leaned in close to her face.

"I'm glad you're here," she whispered.

"Me too."

The two of them sat together in silence. In the bassinet, the baby slept soundly.

Perhaps Jen needed some distraction.

"Hey, guess who's pregnant?" he asked.

"Who?"

"Patty and Matt. She didn't want to say anything while you were missing, but told me a few hours ago. They're about eight weeks along."

Jenny smiled. "That's great. I'm happy for them."

"We've received dozens of requests for media interviews. I hope you don't mind, but I've turned them all down...at least until you're feeling better. "

She nodded.

A hospital worker knocked on the door and proceeded to place a tray of Jello and soup on the table beside the bed.

"Hungry?" he asked.

"I suppose so."

"I'll help you." Tom moved the table close to his wife and began feeding her the soup, then the Jello. She seemed to relish every mouthful.

"You *were* hungry."

Tom was rolling the table away when a nurse called from across the room.

"Mrs. Callahan, I need to take the baby to the nursery for a blood test. She'll only be gone a few minutes."

"Take the baby?" Jen asked. Her already pale face lost its remaining color. She looked at Tom like she wanted him to be her knight in shining armor again. He realized that his wife didn't want the baby out of her sight. And who could blame her?

"Would it be all right for me to come with you?"

"Of course, Mr. Callahan. You're welcome to accompany your baby to the nursery and wait while I perform the test."

Tom knew that statistically the chances of anything happening at this stage of the game were nil, but he appreciated his wife's anxiousness. After all she had experienced, he wanted to do everything in his power to make her comfortable.

"Sure. I'll come with you." Tom looked back at Jen and

winked. "I'll be right back." He followed behind the nurse. Moving into the hall, the nurse spoke with the officer guarding Jen's room. Within a few moments, they started down the hallway, the nurse pushing the bassinet with the baby inside.

* * *

Denise moved with surprising swiftness, considering the accident. She put on her shoes then stepped into the hallway.

She passed numerous metal trolleys and several hospital workers handing out lunches. At a nurse's desk, she asked for directions to the nursery. Following the signs, she arrived at the nursery window. Denise avoided looking in the nursery because she had to concoct a plan first. Besides, she'd have lots of time to look at the baby later.

Exploring the area for a few moments, Denise noticed a hospital worker removing linens from a large closet around the corner and down the hallway. Once she took the baby, she would need a place to regroup before trying to make it out of the hospital. That storage closet would be perfect. But she would also need another room or closet which might act as a decoy. She returned to the area near the nursery. She carefully opened and closed doors until she discovered a small broom closet, which would be ideal for a diversion. She locked the door on the inside, then closed it. Confident that her plan would be foolproof, she made her way back toward the nursery.

She peered through the nursery window and could see no babies inside. She clenched her hands and almost pounded the window. No, she had to control her anger; she couldn't risk bringing attention to herself. Not now. To the right of her, a squealing sound announced the arrival of a nurse, who was rolling a bassinet toward the nursery. Jenny's husband, Tom, followed closely behind. Her heart started to race. The nurse entered the nursery. Jenny's husband said, "How long do you think this will take?"

"No more than five minutes." Tom leaned against the wall and glanced down the hallway toward Denise. She turned and faced the nursery window. If only he would step away.

"I'll be right back. I'm just going over to that vending machine near the window."

Bingo, Denise thought, grinning. She stared closely, her nose touching the glass, trying to read the writing on the card attached to the bassinet. "Callahan, girl." A girl. Jenny had a girl. Denise had been hoping for a girl. *That baby was meant to be mine.*

The nurse on duty prepared a syringe. Tom was inserting coins into the vending machine. The nurse turned her back for a moment. The baby girl, Denise's baby, the one she should've gotten, slept quietly. That was a good sign. This baby would be quiet and easy to steal.

Do it now. Denise leaned in, pushed the nurse onto the floor and quickly scooped up the baby. "Stop!" she heard as she ran down the hallway, clutching the baby to her breast. With all that had happened, Denise thought her chance at motherhood had been ripped away from her. Now, she was just taking back what was rightfully hers.

*   *   *

Jenny set the bowl of Jello down on her bedside table. She wondered when Tom would return with the baby. She nearly jumped at the sound of a loud buzzing alarm. *What in the world is going on?* She sat up in bed and groaned; her tummy still sore. Several nurses and others ran past her room. She heard someone say, "Lock down!" All of a sudden, Jenny had a sick feeling in the pit of her stomach.

*   *   *

Stowing away in the large dark closet, Denise listened to the clambering of people in the hallway. As she had suspected, this was the ideal hiding place. The closet was dark, but she felt her way and moved around some sort of shelving unit. She didn't want to turn the light on in case it drew attention to the closet. Her heart was pounding a mile a minute and her hands shook as she held the baby. In the darkness of the cramped room, Denise could feel the little one moving and making grunting sounds. Then the baby let out a half-cry. Denise frantically stuck her thumb in the infant's mouth and she sucked eagerly. Soon, the baby relaxed against Denise's chest.

* * *

Kathy rushed up to the maternity ward. Alarms were ringing and the hospital was currently in lock down to prevent whomever had taken the Callahan baby from the leaving the hospital. Kathy couldn't believe it when she got the call that the Callahan baby had been taken from the nursery. How could the hospital let this happen?

Tom saw her as soon as she approached the nursery.

"What happened, Tom?" Tom's face had already been drained of its color and, not surprisingly, the poor man looked distraught.

"A lady took our baby. I only caught sight of the back of her. I chased after her, but she disappeared into thin air. She's gone and she took our baby."

"Can you describe her?"

Tom hesitated. "She looked like a patient, with a hospital gown, her head bandaged, maybe short dark hair."

"Thanks, Tom. Now go back and stay with your wife."

He nodded, although Kathy could see that this whole ordeal was weighing down his shoulders.

A group of police officers had already gathered around Kathy. "Go down that hallway. Report anything suspicious. Check every closet and room. The hospital's already in a lock down. She couldn't have gotten far."

* * *

Outside in the hallway, Denise heard an officer shout, "This door's locked!" Another person said, "That door isn't usually locked; it's just a broom closet." Pounding and more shouting followed. The diversion was working. But Denise didn't have time to feel smug. She had to get out before someone found her. She grabbed some linens from the shelf and wrapped the baby in them. She carried the bundle on her hip. She cracked open the door. The cops were huddled in front of the locked broom closet 20 feet away. She quietly stepped into the hallway.

*   *   *

Tom hesitated in front of the nursery before returning to Jen's room. What in God's name was he going to tell his wife? He had gone with the baby to protect her and now she was gone. *Dear God, please bring our baby back to us.* He heard shouting and headed toward the noise.

*   *   *

Kathy and another officer joined the commotion. She reached the group of officers just as they were breaking down the door. "Nothing in here." Kathy groaned and looked down the hallway.

She could see a person, perhaps a patient, carrying a bundle of linen on her hip. Studying her, she saw the patient shuffle quickly along the hallway and practically brushed the wall with her body. The woman rounded another corner. Kathy shouted "Hey, you, stop!"

The woman began to run, knocking carts over so that Kathy had to jump them. Kathy leapt over a cart, grateful that she had been the senior track and field hurdle champion. She prayed the woman wouldn't trip or drop the bundle. At the end of a hallway, Denise stood in front of a tall open window, her head bobbing up and down and her eyes shifting.

Kathy drew her gun. "It's no use. Hand over the baby, Denise."

*   *   *

Denise hadn't come this far to lose her baby now. She would be keeping this baby, no matter what. And if she couldn't have her, no one would.

Using her foot, Denise kicked the screen out and held

the baby toward the open window. "Come any closer and I'll drop her out the window and three floors down. Think she'll survive?"

That stupid lady with the gun had her mouth wide open, but said nothing.

"Put the gun down or I'll throw her. I swear I will."

* * *

"Okay. Okay. I'll do whatever you say. Just don't hurt that baby." Kathy crouched down and placed her gun on the floor.

"Now, you listen to me. Get me a car and a baby seat or I'll kill this baby right now."

"Yes, yes, okay." Kathy took out her cell phone, dialed and began to whisper.

"Hey, hey," Denise yelled. "No whispering."

Speaking more loudly into her cell phone, she said, "She's requesting a car and a baby seat."

"Good," Denise replied. "I want them now or I'll..."

A quick glance revealed that a group of onlookers, mostly nurses and doctors, had gathered behind Kathy. Much to Kathy's dismay, Tom was among them. The poor man looked like he was going to be sick.

She couldn't think of him right now... she had to focus on getting the baby from Denise.

Moments ticked by as the crowd of onlookers increased.

"Where is that baby seat? I want it now!" Denise yelled.

Finally, a male orderly approached Kathy. She sighed with relief. Constable Anderson looked believable dressed as an orderly.

"Here's the car seat, and the police said to tell you a car is waiting downstairs." He stepped forward to place the seat on the ground.

Denise, momentarily distracted by fumbling through the many folds of linen, finally found the sleeping baby. As Constable Anderson jumped on her, Denise screamed, the baby's head now peeking out of the linen. Kathy dove forward and caught the bundle.   Another officer stepped in and restrained the struggling woman.   She was now screaming, "No! No!   It's not fair, it's not fair!   That's my baby!"

Kathy looked down at the baby. She was opening her mouth and starting to whimper.

Tom was beside her in an instant.

"I think this little lady has had enough excitement for the day," Kathy said, handing the baby to her father.

Relief spread across Tom's face as he once again held his newborn daughter.

Thirty-One

On the way back to Jen's room, he and baby Cathy were accompanied by four police officers. *Too much, too little, too late.* Tom could feel his infant daughter's heart beating against his chest. Sergeant Romano remained with the kidnapper, but she told Tom that she would be visiting Jen's room as soon as the woman was processed.

When he reached her room, Jen was sitting up in bed, and looking like she was about to cry. When she saw their baby in his arms, she relaxed against the pillow.

"Tom, I had this horrible feeling that something was wrong."

"Everything's fine."

"What were all those alarms for?"

"Uh..."

"And if everything's fine, why do you look like you've just been through hell."

"Well...the police just discovered that your kidnapper is here, in the hospital."

Jenny gasped. His wife's hands began to shake. "I suppose I should be relieved, but I'm still afraid."

"She's in police custody."

"How? Why?"

"That was the commotion."

"All the alarms?"

He nodded. "She tried to take our baby."

"What?"

"She was caught. The baby is fine." For the time being, Jen didn't need to know that baby Cathy had been in danger.

"I'm so glad I insisted you go with her."

Tom tried to nod, but he was feeling like a failure for letting it all happen. He had only gone to humor Jen, not because he believed something bad could actually happen.

He had been standing right there, within 15 feet of that

woman, and he couldn't stop her. Fathers are supposed to protect their children, to keep them from harm's way. When he first caught a glimpse of her running off with the baby, he was so shocked that he couldn't comprehend the scene. It felt like his feet were nailed to the floor. Of course, when he did finally chase after her, she seemed to have disappeared into thin air.

*   *   *

Fear and anger again welled up inside Jenny. And how would she ever feel safe again?

She glanced at her husband's face. He was quietly holding their baby. "Hey."

"Hey," he winked and made a feeble attempt at a smile. Jen could tell that he was trying to disguise the fact that he was upset.

"What's wrong, Tom?"

He shook his head.

Later, Sergeant Romano visited the room with another officer. Tom stood up and welcomed the two into the room.

The young man accompanying the sergeant looked vaguely familiar. He smiled at her, but she couldn't place where she had seen him or how she knew him. Sergeant Romano glanced at Tom, then stood beside Jenny's bed.

"Hello, Jenny. This officer would like to speak to you."

"Sure."

Sergeant Romano stepped back and the young man inched forward.

"Good to see you again, Jenny." His voice sounded familiar.

"Jen, you remember Jeff Anderson, don't you?" she heard her husband say.

Jenny was sure that her face was flushed. Of course she remembered him. He had changed quite a bit since high school. The skinny, awkward teenage version of Jeff still occasionally haunted her dreams at night. She glanced away.

"Jenny?" She brought her gaze to Jeff's face. He leaned down. "I want to apologize for the heartache I caused you in high school. I hope you will find it in your heart to forgive me."

Jeff's eyes were pleading for forgiveness, expectantly waiting for an answer. If Jenny could even try to forgive Denise, then she could certainly forgive this man who seemed genuinely contrite.

"Yes, I forgive you."

"Constable Anderson is the one who apprehended Denise," offered Tom.

Jeff was smiling, but looking away and shrugging his shoulders like he was modest about his heroism.

"Thank you so much," said Jenny.

"You're very welcome," said Jeff, "and I wanted you to know that my wife and I have been praying for your safe return. I am grateful to God that you and your baby are all right."

"Thank you."

Constable Anderson smiled at her and left the room.

"How about that?" Tom whispered.

"Yes, that was something."

People really do change, Jenny thought.

"Jen?"

"Huh?"

"Sergeant Romano was talking to you," her husband said.

"Oh, sorry. I guess I'm distracted."

"After what you've been through, you're allowed to be distracted," Sergeant Romano offered. "I was just saying that that's all for now. When you're out of the hospital, I'll conduct a video statement with you. When we approach the trial, assuming there is one, the crown attorney will be meeting with you to discuss the case.

"Denise may plead guilty, which will save you the difficulties of being a witness at her trial."

"And if there's no trial and she pleads guilty, will I get a chance to speak to her?"

"Either way, you'll be encouraged to make a victim impact statement at her sentencing. You will be free to say whatever you'd like at that time."

After the officers left, Jenny and Tom sat quietly.

Seeing Jeff again, Jenny felt confident that she would never have another nightmare about the bully who made fun of her in high school. Denise would always be a part of her nightmares, if Jenny didn't somehow gain the courage to face her and to let her know the consequences of what she's done. The victim impact statement would hopefully allow her to do that. But how could she ever forgive Denise, let alone pray for her?

She turned toward her husband, who was still holding their daughter. When he saw Jenny watching him, he tried to lighten the mood by smiling. But the smile came off as a grimace.

"Tom, what's wrong? Please talk to me."

He exhaled, like he had been holding his breath a long time.

"I was right there when she took off with our baby. I froze, couldn't move for a few seconds. I saw that she had turned the corner, but by the time I finally was able to run after her, she had disappeared."

"Oh."

"So now you have it: the father who can't protect his daughter."

"That's not true at all, Tom."

"Deep down, I know that's right, but I... "

Jenny patted the bed. "Come here." He moved to the edge of her bed, the baby between them. She took hold of his hand and kissed it.

*   *   *

Kathy waited in the hallway beside the closed door of Denise's hospital room for the Legal Aid attorney to arrive. After waiting ten minutes, the young man finally showed up, his tie askew, his hair messed and his briefcase flapping open.

"Mr. Kelly?"

"Yes, and you would be Sergeant Romano?"

She held out her hand which Mr. Kelly graciously shook. "I'm here to speak to your client."

"Get in line. I haven't spoken to her yet. Allow me a moment to speak to her before you do."

"That would be fine."

The young man went into the room and closed the door. Kathy figured that it would be a while before she would be allowed to speak to Denise, so she lifted out her Blackberry and she dialed her husband's number. He answered on the second ring.

"Hey, how's it going? Sorry I haven't called. I've been a little busy."

"Don't sweat it. I hear from the news that your victim's been found and she and her baby are going to make it."

"It's great news."

"When will you be home?"

"I've got a few things to wrap up. Hopefully I'll be home later tonight."

"Danny and I are proud of you, Sergeant," her husband said.

"Thanks."

Just then, Mr. Kelly came out of Denise's room and motioned for her to come in. "Gotta go, see you later...love you." She hung up before her husband said goodbye.

Denise Kramer was lying in the hospital bed, her hands shackled to the bed, her eyes closed, and Kathy was moved more by pity than any other emotion. Hours ago, Jenny Callahan was most likely in the same position as her captor, chained to a bed. For the moment, Denise was quiet.

Kathy leaned down and spoke. "Mrs. Kramer?"

The woman drowsily opened her eyes and turned towards Kathy. Then Denise's eyes flew open and her eyebrows narrowed. She boldly looked in Kathy's direction, her eyes defiant and scowling, a piercing stare.

"Mrs. Kramer, we have evidence that you've been stalking Jenny with the intent of stealing her baby. We suspect that you stole drugs from the Sutherland Veterinary Hospital. We have evidence that you kept Jenny in a cottage on Farewell Lane near Cedar Lake. There is a great deal of evidence against you. If you cooperate, perhaps the crown attorney can offer a plea deal. That is, after your psychiatric evaluation."

* * *

That lady sergeant thinks she's so smug. But she's the one who stopped her from taking the baby. If it wasn't for her, Denise would be in another town, perhaps another province, with a baby to call her own.

Denise was in no mood for talking. Everything was gone. And now she would never have a baby.

The Legal Aid attorney, a good looking but clumsy young man, encouraged her to cooperate with police. This was a high profile crime, the lawyer had said, and it would "go well with the police if you cooperated with them."

Even that lady sergeant said she should cooperate. Not that Denise cared about anything the cop said.

Cooperate? Like she was supposed to cooperate with the shrink they brought in to see if she was of "sound mind." Well, if she wasn't of "sound mind," how did they expect her to cooperate?

A nurse came in and gave her some pills. The stupid pills were making her want to sleep. How was she supposed to get any sleep with the restraints on her hands and feet?

Thirty-Two

Before Chris got out of the van, she helped Chloe out of her booster seat. Nana and Dad pulled them all close as she heard the clicks of the cameras and the people yelling at them. Her dad told her there would be lots of reporters at the hospital so they tried to sneak in the back door near the emergency room, but there were lots of people there too. Chris was happy and relieved that her mom was okay, and that her new baby sister was okay.

"Come on, kids," Dad said, as he and Nana huddled them as they hurried them in through the hospital's doors.

* * *

A thunder of footsteps outside her hospital room made Jenny smile. She could always tell when her children were approaching and could hear their sweet chatter.

A chorus of "Mommy, Mommy" rang out as they rushed to her bed. Jenny wished she could pull them all onto her lap and gather them into her arms, but she was still weak and her abdomen remained sore.

"How are my angels doing?"

"Oh, we're fine, Mommy, now that we've found you," answered Chloe.

"I did pee on the potty!" Caleb shouted.

"Good for you! You're getting to be such a big boy."

Cassie and Callie came up close to Jenny's face. "We missed you, Mom."

Jenny's mom walked to the other side of the bed and leaned down. She whispered, "I was so worried about you." She had tears in her eyes and hugged Jenny tightly.

"I know, Mom."

Chris stayed beside Tom and she was avoiding eye contact with Jenny. "Chris?"

"Hmmm?"

"Come, sit on my bed. I want to talk to you."

Tom accompanied their daughter closer to Jenny's bed, then helped his wife sit up. The other children were now fawning over the newest addition to their family.

"She's so small, Mom," Chloe said.

"Can I hold her?" Caleb asked.

"In a little bit," Dad answered.

Jenny stared at her oldest daughter, who was avoiding eye contact. "Are you all right, Chris?"

The girl kept her eyes focused on her feet.

"I'm going to be fine now," Jenny said quietly.

"I know, but this is my fault."

Tom and Jenny both said "No, no." Jenny reached out and caressed her daughter's cheek. "Why do you think it's your fault?"

"Because I shouldn't have insisted you come to the bus stop early. I should have been able to walk my sisters home from the bus stop. I should've been a big girl." Chris started to sob. "Oh, honey," Jenny whispered.

Tom crouched down to his daughter's eye level. "This is not your fault, Chris, not in any way, shape or form. The woman who kidnapped Mommy is to blame. This has nothing to do with you."

"Daddy's right. This is absolutely not your fault."

"I was so scared for you, Mommy."

"I know, Chris. I was scared too. I didn't think I would ever see you guys again."

"I'm so glad you're okay." Chris straightened and wiped her eyes.

"Besides..." Tom began, "you will be receiving half of the reward money, $12,500."

"Really?"

"You bet."

"Wow. What will I do with all that money?"

"We're putting it into a college fund for you."

"Okay. Who will be getting the other half?"

"A witness named Frank Heff."

"Oh."

Tom took her hand and walked her to the bassinet. "Come see your baby sister."

Chris turned to look at her baby sister.

Tom leaned down and whispered in his oldest daughter's ear. "She looks just like you when you were born."

"Really?" She asked, looking at her mom.

"You bet."

Chris inched closer to the bassinet. The baby was awake and staring at the little faces surrounding her. "She sure is cute," Chris observed. "Just like having my own twin, like Callie and Cassie, huh?"

Jenny glanced at Tom with a knowing expression. He leaned down and whispered, "Maybe some day we'll tell her that her twin is in heaven?"

"Perhaps."

Sergeant Romano knocked at the door. "Is there some sort of party in here or something?"

"Come on in, Sergeant," Jenny called.

Tom said, "Now that you mention it, we did have a party planned." Tom winked at the kids and rushed into the hallway. He returned with a huge balloon arrangement. Tom began singing and everyone joined in. "Happy Birthday to you, Happy Birthday to you, Happy Birthday Dear Mommy, Happy Birthday to you!"

Jenny was grinning from ear to ear. With all that had happened and confusion in her mind about which day it was, she had forgotten that her birthday was close. "It's the 11th?" she asked her mom, who winked at her. A milestone birthday, her 30th.

The kids surrounded her, giving her small wrapped presents. "Open mine, Mom."

"No, mine first."

Their high-pitched voices grew louder, with each child trying to speak over the others. The baby started to cry. Tom picked her up and rocked her back and forth. Jenny sat back and savored the moment. *Thank you, God, for bringing me back to my family.*

Epilogue

Five months later

Inside a private room in the courthouse, the clicking of Jenny's boots echoed on the tile floor as she paced. Most of the reporters were in the courtroom covering the sentencing hearing of Denise Kramer. She had decided not to be present in the courtroom for the entire hearing. Instead, she chose to wait with Tom. Cathy was fussy, ready for her afternoon nap and wanting to nurse.

Jenny wore her best Sunday clothes, an angora sweater and a blue skirt.

Sergeant Romano had given her the thumbs up a few moments ago, indicating that she would be accompanying Jenny to the courtroom in a moment. She was nervous and her hands were already shaking.

Since the kidnapping, Sergeant Romano had called Jenny frequently to ask how she was doing and if there was anything she could do for her. She seemed genuinely interested in Jenny's welfare, not just someone who was being paid to follow up a case.

Earlier this week, the sergeant had visited Jenny and the two of them had spent over an hour discussing her victim impact statement. She had informed Jenny that Denise would be pleading guilty to the lesser charges of kidnapping and forcible confinement instead of kidnapping and attempted murder. Denise had been committed to a psychiatric hospital for one month while being evaluated, was judged to be competent to stand trial, treated for several mental conditions, then confined to the provincial jail for the past two months. Although she had agreed to a plea and approximate sentence length, the judge still had the authority to hand down a harsher penalty.

Up until the time Sergeant Romano had called her

about the plea agreement, the nightmares had lessened, but the last few days were filled with restless sleeps and reliving her time in captivity. Part of her didn't want to ever see Denise's face again. But Jenny knew that it was necessary to confront her captor or she would never truly heal. So she had spent the last few days preparing her victim impact statement.

Jenny continued to pray for Denise and to pray for the grace to forgive her. On good days, she actually felt the stirrings of forgiveness. On not-so-good days, the fear and anger remained.

Sergeant Romano opened the door and motioned for Jenny to come forward. Jenny's hands continued to shake. Tom was now leaning against the wall, holding their daughter, rocking her from side to side, his fingers flat against her small back. He winked at her and mouthed "Good luck."

Jenny followed Sergeant Romano into the hallway. A few reporters approached them, but Sergeant Romano motioned them away. Jenny held her chin high. Entering the courtroom, her written statement clutched in her hand, Jenny heard murmurs and felt the stares of the packed courtroom. As she drew closer, she smiled at the crown attorney, an older balding gentleman in a black court gown. He ushered her toward the microphone.

Before speaking, Jenny faced the defense table. The defense lawyer wore a black court gown, but his hair looked like it hadn't been combed in days — or maybe that was the style. In the prisoner box between the two counsel tables, Denise's head was down, her eyes staring at her clasped hands. She wore a brown and white sweater and brown pants.

Jenny cleared her throat, then leaned into the microphone. At first, she spoke to the judge, her voice soft and trembling.

"Your Honor, I would like to thank you for the

opportunity to speak at this sentencing hearing. Five months ago, I was kidnapped by Denise Kramer and held against my will and almost lost my life. My husband nearly lost his wife and my children, their mother. My baby could have died.

"Because of her actions, I nearly bled to death and it was necessary for me to have a hysterectomy." She took a deep breath before continuing.

"It will be months before my full strength and energy returns. I have developed allergies.

"I am afraid to close my eyes. I am afraid to let my baby or any of my children out of my sight."

Jenny turned and again faced Denise, whose head was still lowered and avoiding eye contact. "Denise, you may not have succeeded in taking my baby, but you succeeded in stealing a part of my identity that I won't ever get back: my fertility. What you took from me was very precious, something that I respected as a gift from God."

There was so much more that Jenny wanted to say. She wanted to share with her that she felt sorry for her, and that she was sad that Denise couldn't have any kids, but that maybe, in her case, that was best. She wanted to remind Denise that most infertile women don't resort to stealing someone else's baby. Jenny's own mother waited a long time to adopt Jenny.

"Mrs. Callahan?" the judge asked. "Do you have anything further to say?"

Facing the judge, she replied, "Yes, I do, Your Honor." She turned again toward Denise and drew in a breath when she realized that Denise was staring back. There were so many emotions whirling around in her mind: anger, fear, sadness, resentment. But facing Denise that day, Jenny also knew that it was important for her own healing process to say four words.

"I forgive you, Denise."

Jenny had always planned to say those words, but they were harder words to say than she had imagined.

Denise's face remained expressionless, almost neutral.

Jenny finally turned and faced the judge. "Thank you."

"Thank *you*, Mrs. Callahan," said the judge, a middle-aged, balding man with kind eyes and a pleasant smile. "You are a remarkable young woman and we're all thankful that you survived."

Jenny nodded then made her way to a seat beside Sergeant Romano.

"Mrs. Kramer, do you have anything to say before I pronounce your sentence?"

The defense attorney stood and motioned for Denise to stand. It was quiet for a minute or so. Finally Jenny heard a sound, but had to strain to hear it.

"Your Honor," Denise said.

As Jenny listened to her voice, she was struck by how soft-spoken yet unemotional her voice sounded, almost robotic.

"I. . .sincerely regret my actions."

Jenny slumped back against the seat. What sort of apology was that? And was it even an apology?

"Thank you. I sentence the defendant to 20 years in jail for the crime of kidnapping and forcible confinement of Jennifer Callahan."

Jenny exhaled. The whole ordeal was now over.

* * *

A female prison guard led Denise away, the woman's firm grasp on her upper arm urging her forward. Denise's hands were now shackled in front of her. Twenty years in prison. The number didn't mean much to her. She didn't feel anything. She slept most of the time, taking pills constantly, sleeping some more, going to the bathroom.

When Jenny said "I forgive you," Denise shrugged. That wasn't important. Either way, she would be going to jail.

Her lawyer told her that she should say "I sincerely regret my actions."

She tried to mean it. Really she did. But what she most regretted was that she didn't succeed in taking Jenny's baby. Every time she saw a baby on TV, that overwhelming need to have a child poked its head through the unemotional layer the doctors created by giving her all those pills. Who did they think they were fooling? She had taken therapeutic drugs many years ago and the stupid pills made her a different person. *I'm still here, deep inside.* Someday, after Denise gained the trust of the prison officials, she would stop taking her pills and plan her escape.

* * *

It was quiet in the courtroom and Jenny could hear the distant sound of her wailing baby in the room down the hallway. Her baby's first cries after waking always sounded so distressed. She excused herself and hurried down the aisle. The court clerk opened the door and allowed her to exit. In the hallway, several reporters approached her and she dodged them. She finally reached the room and found that Tom was bouncing and rocking the baby. However, Cathy wanted no part of it. Jenny gathered her into her arms. She sat on the nearest chair, lifted her blouse and began to nurse. She felt Tom kiss the top of her head.

"How'd it go?"

"Okay, I guess."

"Good."

As the baby gulped, her tiny hand caressed Jenny's breast, her small mouth sighing as she nursed. Jenny had never heard any sound so sweet.

Author's notes/Disclaimer

Placenta previa is a life-threatening condition which, for both the safety of the mother and health of the baby, usually necessitates a Caesarean section. The story is completely the product of the author's imagination and in no way does the author present the ideal situation for a woman with placenta previa to have a vaginal home birth.

Sutherland is a fictional town and any resemblance to any other city or town in Ontario is entirely coincidental. As well, Queen Victoria Hospital is a fictional hospital.

Acknowledgments

I am indebted to Regina Doman, Andrew Schmiedicke and Christopher Blunt for their invaluable editorial assistance.

A special thanks to my editor, Cheryl Thompson, and to my team of proofreaders: Sarah Loten, Karen Murphy Corr and Ginger Regan.

And with grateful appreciation to the following people, who helped in a number of ways: my husband, James Hrkach, for discussing various plotlines and characters, and also for designing and photographing the front cover; Linda Barton, for her assistance with veterinary terms and procedures; Constable Colin Slight of Ontario Provincial Police Department for assisting me with police terms and procedures; Maureen Sullivan-Bentz, RN, for helping with medical terms; Brian and Karen Boese, for allowing us to photograph the cabin (located on their property) for the cover photograph. And, last but not least, thank you to the following people for reading various manuscripts and offering helpful feedback: Kathy Cassanto, Ben Hrkach, Ginger Regan, Ingrid Waclawik and Michelle Sinasac.

About the Author

Ellen Gable is a wife and mother living in Pakenham, Ontario. She is a freelance writer and author. Her second novel, "In Name Only," has been an Amazon Kindle Top 100 bestseller. In 2010, "In Name Only" won the Gold Medal in Religious Fiction in the IPPY Awards (and was the first Catholic novel to win this award.) Her first novel, "Emily's Hope" won an Honorable Mention Award in the 2006 IPPY Awards. Her third book, "Come My Beloved: Inspiring Stories of Catholic Courtship" was released earlier this year. All four of her books have received the Catholic Writers' Guild Seal of Approval.

She has had articles published in various magazines and websites, and currently is a columnist for Amazing Catechists.com, CatholicMom.com, a reviewer for Catholic Fiction.net, and a frequent contributor to Catholic Exchange. Her website is www.ellengable.com.

Ellen and her husband, James Hrkach, also currently create a Catholic cartoon called "Family Life," which appears in Family Foundations magazine. They have been a Certified NFP Teaching Couple Specialist for the Couple to Couple League since 1984 and have been working in Marriage Preparation since 1983.

Ellen is always interested in hearing reader feedback. Email her at info@fullquiverpublishing.com.

www.stealingjenny.com
www.fullquiverpublishing.com